TAKEN BY THE BILLIONAIRE

A BWWM Romance

by Shani Greene-Dowdell

ISBN: 978-1717945846
Library of Congress: Applied For

Published by Imperial Publishing House, a subsidiary of Nayberry Publications, Opelika, AL.
For copyright issues, including permissions for use or to report improper use, contact Shani Dowdell, 334-787-0733.

I would like to thank all of my faithful Nayberry readers for your extraordinary patience as I finished this book! I truly hope you enjoy it.

Shani

PROLOGUE

Tess

My wedding day was the happiest day of my life. I felt like a princess stepping into queendom when I strapped on my off-white satin wedding gown and strappy heels. The day I became Mrs. Tess Knox was whimsical, a day filled with magic.

"Marissa, I can't believe this is happening," I said to my best friend and confidant. She had been by my side since forever. She'd stuck by me when other friends and lovers left me high and dry. When I lost the two most important people in my life, Marissa was there, my down by law rider. If there was one thing I could depend on in life, I could depend on her loyalty and love for me, and that meant the world to me.

I needed her steadiness. I was used to things changing up and people leaving me. My parents died in their late fifties, Mom succumbing to a stroke from overwhelming grief only a few days after the burial of Dad. Therefore, Marissa Murray and my soon-to-be husband, Amiri Knox, had been the two constants in my life. I loved them both deeply. I depended on them more than anything. Both brought much-needed stability into my life. Amiri, my lover of all times. Marissa, my unwavering rock to lean on. With them by my side, I faced a brutal world with sheer confidence.

"It's definitely happening friend. You're getting married to Amiri Knox's fine ass," Marissa said. "He's the man of your dreams, and everything looks to be working out for you."

Marissa stared out of the window. Her voice wafted away with the sun's rays. Her bouquet rested on the sill beside her tiny caramel-colored hands. My gorgeous friend was thinking about her own love life. She always did. Her latest, Dustin, ran off after he got the goods. She was back to square one, trying to sift through the many players and misfits out there in the dating pool.

"Thanks, Marissa. One day soon, these men are going to realize they're sleeping on a great woman. They'll recognize you're the most beautiful, eligible bachelorette in the city," I assured her as I stared into her hooded obsidian-colored eyes with rich darkness that accented her round face perfectly.

"I wish they would realize it today," she said softly, then sighed. "But I don't see that happening any time soon. Instead, you're the one looking like you've been cut out of the Saffire Wedding Magazine, and that's all I want you to focus on today. Being gorgeous for your husband. You look absolutely fantabulous." She forced a smile, despite the obvious turmoil stirring inside of her because of her own troubling reality. I ached for my friend to find someone to make her as happy as I was that day.

Just as she finished her sentence, the sparkling glow of princess-cut diamonds that trimmed my neckline blinded my vision in the mirror. My future husband insisted upon nothing but the best for my bridal jewelry, down to the last detail. Beige satin draping covered the chairs and tables in my dressing room with the same diamond pattern that brought the cathedral to life. My wedding was larger than life with no expenses spared at Amiri's urging.

"Marissa, thank you for being here for me," I said, shaking with emotion. Up until I met Amiri, she really was all I had.

"Oh, chile, save that noise. I'll always be by your side. You and Amiri couldn't get rid of me to save your lives," she joked.

"No, I mean it. I know this sounds cliché, but you really are my only family. That's why I'm glad you're here to not only be my maid of honor but also to give me away," I said.

"Just know that if I didn't think Amiri was in love with you, I would not be giving my best friend away. But he loves you, and that I can't deny," she said, her forehead wrinkling and lips quivering. I could plainly that see she was overwhelmed with sad emotion. She tried her best to cover it with a smile.

"Awe!" I spread my arms wide for a hug. "Come here, girl." We met each other halfway across the room, and I gathered my best friend up in my arms. I wrapped my arms around her waist. "Today is special," I said.

"And, we'll rejoice and be glad in it," she said along with me. "And we're going to get tore up from the floor up at the reception," she added wiping her tears away.

"Yassss! The DJ has my hit list, so it's going to be a turned-up reception for sure. You ready to hit the Quan for our group dance?" I asked, dancing in my gown to hype my friend up about all the dance moves we practiced.

"Tess, you're always the life of the party. It's okay to just break down and cry if you want to," Marissa said as she finished helping me get dressed. "I'll redo your eyes if you need me to."

"I don't have a reason to cry. I truly feel like I'm about to make the best decision of my life. I'm marrying the love of my life, the man who stole my heart, snatched it right out of my chest, and claimed it as his own. I have you here by my side. I don't see any other option but to be happy," I smiled, as my body tingled all over with magnificent joy.

Marissa lifted my train and spun it around. "Well, let's go then."

I walked to the doorway, then turned and looked back at her. In a few minutes, I would be gaining a husband and a new extended family, but Marissa's unconditional love would forever be in my heart, and she would forever be my real sister, blood or not.

Chills ran over me when I floated down the aisle approaching my soon-to-be husband. Yes, that handsome hunk of man was about to be mine...all mine.

We were so alive and fulfilled when the minister finally pronounced us husband and wife. But nothing, and I do mean nothing, made me prouder than when my best friend stepped down from her place as my maid of honor to give me away. I never imagined her gorgeous smile that day hid something deep inside that would ruin me.

When my friend's dark secret was finally revealed, it would leave me struggling to salvage the crumpled pieces of my heart, all because of a salacious affair that would leave me with nowhere to turn, no one to trust.

CHAPTER ONE

Tess

One Year Later

I talked myself out of following him five times already. I mean, what self-respecting woman pops up at places their husband is supposed to be just to see what he's doing?

A wife who doesn't want to play the fool, that's who, I answered my own question. Unable to clear my mind, I put down the book I was unsuccessfully reading and got out of bed. Amiri had been coming home at all times of night, smelling of alcohol mixed with sweet perfume. He told me not to worry. He said women who attended late office meetings gave him goodbye hugs, leaving their fragrance behind. But, I didn't trust him anymore. My lack of trust was cause enough to worry.

It was hard to believe the man who rushed home and playfully harassed me for sex every night for months had suddenly forgotten his way home. He wasn't hard up for sex or to spend time with me these days either.

"I gotta go see what he's doing," I said to the lonely bedroom that used to be so full of life. Our life. Beautiful memories once permeated every corner of our beautifully decorated bedroom.

Proof that Amiri was working would settle my mind. My gut told me what my husband was doing, but I needed concrete answers. I needed to see the truth with my own two eyes. Then, I would know I wasn't dealing with a low-down lying cheater.

After sliding into a pair of jeans and a black sweater, I slipped into my black running shoes. Standing in the mirror looking like I was about to go on a black ops mission, I stared at the honey-colored oval face, high cheeks, and deep-set eyes looking back at me. *What are you going to do if you find out he's cheating?* I wondered to myself.

"Shoot his ass where he stands," I answered that thought in a bitter tone. My usually serene features twisted into an angry scowl. "If Amiri knows what's good for him, he'll be at work like he says he is, and everything will be peachy."

I walked out of my bedroom door and down my long hallway. To everyone who knew me, I was a good girl. The queen of charity. An uplifter. You know, the nice girl who's always volunteering to take care of others, the girl who thinks of her needs last. Yeah, I was that girl. I would do anything for anybody, but everyone had a snapping point.

There may not even be a reason to snap though, I thought. I reminisced the deep love Amiri and I shared, which made me think there had to be a logical explanation for his change in behavior. Surely, he wasn't seeing another woman. There had to be another reason for his absence. I mean, why would he cheat? We loved each other too hard, too completely. I was the totality of him, and he the totality of me. What could another woman give him that was not hot and ready at home?

I dialed his number. Once again, it went straight to voicemail. I grabbed my purse off the living room sofa. Inside was my nickel plated nine-millimeter on safety inside a pouch. Amiri insisted I carry it with me at all times for my safety. Tonight, I prayed for his safety. If I found him doing what my gut kept doubling back to, he would need all the prayer he could get, and so would I.

I walked out the front door determined to put my mind to rest about Amiri being with another woman. The ride to Lexington Cooper Enterprises was short. When I drove into the parking lot and saw his car, I let out a sigh of relief.

See, there's nothing to worry about. I'm just being paranoid, I scolded internally. I found a parking space close to the entrance. It was a little after 8:00 p.m. so almost everyone was gone for the day. Guilt raked through me as I thought about the accusations my mind had wielded at Amiri.

Maybe I should give him a little late-night office fun just for thinking the way I did.

I got out of my car and took the elevator to his floor. I strolled through the quiet building like I owned the place. Since it was nearly empty, a smile crept upon my lips. I had a confident stride as I approached Amiri's office thinking about seeing his handsome face again. That confidence was cut short when I heard voices on the other side of his office door.

"Dang, he's not alone," I fumed because the plan I'd cooked up on the way in had been foiled. Amiri's meeting was still going on.

"You're hilarious," I heard him say. Then, Amiri let out a slew of giggles. Yes, my husband was inside his office giggling late into the evening.

What's so funny that keeps him in this office all night? I wondered. The conversation he was entertaining sounded like everything but company business.

I stood a few feet away from the door and listened further. I heard a woman's voice. She spoke too softly to make out what she was saying. However, it was clear she was saying something that thrilled the hell out of Amiri. I stood there, four minutes to be exact, and then the laughter stopped.

"Oh, Amiri, you're a fucking beast. I love it when we're together," the woman's voice purred out loud enough for me to hear her this time.

At that very moment, the Earth stopped spinning on its axis. That voice...her voice. It became distinctively clear to me. My heart sank into my stomach. I felt like I'd been sucker-punched right in the ticker. *Please God, don't...don't let this be real.*

I got up the nerve to push the door open. I had to see it with my own eyes. The silhouette of a voluptuous woman with long ringlets falling from her head and touching her shoulders stuck me in my eyes like needles. Her caramel-colored thighs spread wide across Amiri's desk as she moaned out his name.

Amiri kneeled between her thighs eager to drink from her fountain of deception.

"Marissa, how could you?" I screamed, cutting off the moan that was about to escape her throat as his tongue made contact with her flesh.

Her eyes popped open wide. She looked at me with unspeakable shock and shame on her face. Marissa sat up straight on the desk and started tugging at her skirt.

"Tess, I'm so so——"

"Don't you dare try to cover your body now, you homewrecking bitch! And no, don't you think about apologizing. You're my best friend. What in the hell are you doing in here with Amiri, Marissa?" The sight of their half naked bodies and the looks of guilt on their faces ripped at my heart. "Oh, my God, I can't believe you two. Oh, my God!"

"Baby, it's not what it looks like," Amiri found the gumption to chime in, bringing my attention to him. His hand went to his mouth, I assumed, to wipe away Marissa's juices. By this time, he was standing with a big, brown erection pointed directly toward me. I was thoroughly disgusted. "Marissa came by to talk about a problem she's been having, and um——"

"And, let me guess, licking her pussy is the best advice you had to offer?"

Marissa's mouth started moving. She sang like a canary bird. She told the tale she should have told me a long time ago.

"Tess, I'm sorry. I'm so sorry. I never meant for you to find out like this, but Amiri and I have been sleeping together since you got married a year ago. I wanted to tell you, but I couldn't find the words to say to you." She paused and looked into Amiri's eyes, then added, "We're in love."

"In love?" I yelled incredulously. Each passing moment brought more pain, more shock. "How could you be in love with my husband? Marissa, I invited you into our home. You've sipped my wine, laughed, talked, and even cried with me. And, the whole time you were fucking my husband? I can't believe this shit. In *love*." She made it sound so simple to be in love with her best friend's husband, as if this was something women did all the time.

The tiny voice in my mind that spoke to my worse instincts grew louder. It started as a whisper, but as I stood there looking at the two people who held my heart in public, yet held each other in private, the sound grew louder until it was raging. *Kill both their asses. Kill them. Make them feel your pain. They don't deserve to live after hurting you like this.* The voice was so loud that the next thing I knew I had reached into my purse and put my hand on my pistol.

Unaware of the turmoil brewing within me, Amiri turned to Marissa and gave a pitiful attempt at trying to sound innocent.

"Why're you lying on me, Marissa? This is the first time you seduced me, and it will be the last. I keep telling you that I love my wife, but you keep coming on to me. This has to end right here, right now. Don't come back to my office, and stop preying on the temptations of my flesh," he said.

"Amiri Knox!" Marissa huffed. "I know you're not going there with me. You know what we have shared is deep. Don't try to brush it under the rug just because she's here." Her voice fell into the depths of her throat as she spoke. Her admission did not deter Amiri.

"Marissa, this infatuation you have for me has gone too far. I would have never touched you if you hadn't kept coming on to me," he said, condemning their affair once more.

Amiri's brown orbs flashed Marissa a quick look, which I did not miss. He silently begged her to let him do the talking. He wanted her to let him survive his lies and deceit with the hopes that I would forgive him, and they could go back to hiding their affair at pretend late-night office meetings and wherever else they hooked up. However, nothing he said tonight would ever suffice. Things could never go back to the way they once were.

"Shut up, both of you. Just stop!" I turned to him and wept. "Amiri, I trusted you. I loved you."

He took a step toward me, and I snapped. I pulled my gun from my purse in full view and cocked the hammer back.

"Why? Tell me why I shouldn't put a bullet through your heart and break your heart like you broke mine?" I asked, not caring about the consequences. All I had in this world was my friend and my husband, and I'd been betrayed by both in one swoop.

Amiri took two steps toward me with his hands in the air.

"Tess, I made a mistake. I shouldn't have gotten this close to Marissa, but I swear to you it's not worth anyone dying," Amiri reasoned.

"What about me? This feels like death, Amiri. You just wiped her juices from your lips. My only friend left in the world is sleeping with my husband."

"I don't want her like that, Tess. It was just a moment of temptation. I can fix this. We can get us back."

He took another step toward me. My finger trembled against the trigger.

"A temptation that went on for a year, Amiri? That's not temptation. That's something you wanted, knowing it would break us. You can't explain it away," I cried out.

"Amiri, you might as well tell her everything. She deserves to know the truth," Marissa butted in.

"Be quiet, Marissa."

"No. Look at what our lies are doing to her. She's about to break down, Amiri. We have to come clean about the way we feel," Marissa said.

"Shut up, Marissa!" Amiri spat through gritted teeth. "Let me handle my wife."

"Tess, a few hours ago, Amiri told me it should've been us that got married," Marissa said as tears burst out of her eyes. "Tess, I have mistreated you and for that, I'm sorry. But, he's always wanted me, and I have wanted him. It should have been us that got married. He should be my husband."

"Is this true that you two have always wanted each other, even while we were dating?" I asked Amiri.

Amiri glared at Marissa, then turned to me. Venom shot from my eyes toward his cheating ones.

"Amiri and I…we slept together on your wedding night," Marissa blurted out, adding fuel to the fire. Any hope of a reconciliation doused with her admission.

"Amiri, our wedding night? Our fucking wedding night, Amiri?" I hurled his dirty deed at him along with a bullet that went flying by his head. It felt like the trigger was squeezing itself as my temper boiled over. I had no control over whether either of them lived or died, as I wildly aimed and shot at him.

"I wanted to go to Paris for our wedding night, but you said we couldn't go. We had to stay in Atlanta. You said you had important business that week, so our Paris trip was put off, and we still haven't taken that trip. Well, now I know why." I kept yelling as I squeezed the trigger again. "You're too busy sleeping with Marissa!"

"I didn't sleep with her on our wedding night, Tess," Amiri said, holding his arm out in front of him as if that action could guard against the stray bullets I sent flying in his direction. Amiri turned to Marissa with a look on his face that begged Marissa to help him out. "Marissa, you know I slept with my wife on my wedding night. I don't know why you're lying," he said to her.

"And then, you came to me," Marissa admitted with a look of shame in her eyes. She turned to me. "While I was doing it, I only thought about my own feelings and how much I cared for Amiri. Never once did I consider how bad this would hurt you. Tess, I'm sorry, but on your wedding night I had a suite at the W too. When you went to sleep, Amiri came to my room."

The look in my husband's eyes as Marissa revealed the truth sent me spiraling out of control. He was guilty as charged. Why didn't I put two and two together back then? Maybe I could have done something to stop this night from happening. Maybe I could have stopped my heart from breaking into a zillion tiny particles. Maybe I could have stopped this murder spree that would end with me wearing an orange jumpsuit the rest of my life.

Amiri was always extra friendly with Marissa. She introduced us by setting us up on a blind date. Most of our date nights, we invited Marissa, whether she had a date or not. Lately, she'd been unable to keep a man, and Amiri had harsh criticism for every man she brought around. He often left me at home to help Marissa when her car broke down, when her plumbing was out, or when she needed furniture moved. Whatever my friend, supposedly sister, needed, I had no qualms about it. I trusted them both completely until tonight when the proof of their betrayal rained down on me like missiles.

I thought about the way Marissa dressed with her breasts spilling out of her shirts. How she talked kinky around Amiri while making the suggestions that I do certain sexual positions for him. My husband had a poker face, so he never appeared interested in her. He'd only stopped acting interested in my advances lately. That was my clue that something was wrong. The whole scheme registered in my mind, playing like a movie reel over and over, as I stood there determining which one of them to kill first.

Amiri's dark, coiled hair was cut low on the sides and curled into perfection at the top. He had a freshly manicured beard

I used to love to feel grazing my back as we made love. His silky, chocolate brown skin would make Idris Elba jealous. All of that once made him look delicious to me. Yet, it all appalled me as his tall frame inched toward me.

"Don't take one more step toward me, or I'll actually aim correctly the next time and shoot you where you stand. I hate you, Amiri! I hate you for doing this to me. For making me feel insecure enough to have to come here looking for you, because you won't come home. For sleeping with the only family I have left, my friend, who's not even my friend anymore. If you didn't love me, why did you marry me? If you did love me, why would you cross the line with Marissa, of *all* people? She was my only family. You could have slept with any woman in the world. Why would you ruin our friendship?" I questioned.

The thought of their bodies entangled in passionate moments painted a picture that would forever be implanted in my mind. This could never be undone. No friend would betray me like this.

"I'm sorry, Tess. I do still love you," Marissa said and started sniffling, which brought my attention back to her. "I just, I guess, I was selfish, but—"

I aimed the gun at her.

"You can keep your apologies and your love. How dare you stand your low-down ass in here and cry? You gave me away at my wedding, and now you're screwing my husband at his job. I should be the one crying," I screamed at the top of my lungs.

I was certain the deranged look in my eyes (because I felt deranged) let Marissa know her friend was long gone. The woman standing before her would flatline her in a second. I couldn't explain why I felt so irrational, but I truly was one beat away from a double homicide.

"Please, please don't shoot me. Let my baby live," Marissa said, and the same tiny, caramel-colored hand that fastened my wedding gown eased down to a small baby bump.

My eyes widened.

My heart burst open.

A sea of hatred poured into each chamber.

My world went red.

Every part of my body tensed.

My fingers tightened around the trigger and squeezed.

The gun fell out of my trembling hand.

Amiri dove at me, tackling me to the ground.

I punched his chest over and over.

"I hate you. I hate you. I hate you…" I screamed.

Marissa fell to the floor weeping.

Pain raked through my body, a feeling worse than anything I'd ever felt. I had no clue of where to go from there. I most certainly couldn't return to life as usual. I had lost everything.

CHAPTER TWO

Tess

My phone sang *A Couple of Forevers* over and over, as I walked out of Lexington Cooper Enterprises in a crazed trance. Marissa's acknowledgment of sleeping with Amiri on our wedding night, and now carrying his child, made me regret ever knowing her. I felt betrayed, unloved and murderous as I floated through the parking deck. I didn't stop to check to see if the last bullet I sent flying in Marissa's direction hit its target. After her body hit the floor, I wished I could have squeezed the trigger once more while aiming at Amiri, but the chamber was empty, and the gun fell out of my hands. Amiri tackled me to the ground. I punched him over and over again. Finally, I struggled my way free.

"You should check on your girlfriend," I said to him.

He let me go and turned to look at Marissa. She still lay on the ground crying and holding her stomach. The distraction allowed me to escape Amiri's grasp, get to my feet, and leave out of his office.

Once I reached my car, I stood at the door trying to will my clouded mind to turn the key. I felt crazy. I felt lost. I felt unloved. For the life of me, I couldn't do the simple task of opening my car door.

"Shit!" I gave up, laying an arm on the car and leaning my head against it. The tears came quick and relentlessly, like a waterfall. Feeling low and dejected, I was alone in that parking lot.

All the sanity and dignity I once had was left in the building in front of me. I walked in with self-respect mere minutes ago and left devoid of anything I used to be. I needed to get out of that public place and go somewhere private to break down. I had to think. I swiped my eyes to clear the fog, pressed the button on my keychain, and the doors unlocked, finally.

"Are you okay?" a concerned-looking, tall and burly white man who unfolded from a tiny Corvette asked. He was medium built with a light-golden skin tone. He had a compassionate look in his eyes that put me at ease about him approaching me.

"I'm fine," I replied.

"I was getting out of my car and noticed you running out of the building. I saw you crying and trying to open your door. Is someone following you?" he asked.

"I said I'm fine," I said dismissively.

"It's kind of late for you to be out here alone," he continued to badger me.

"*I'm fine.* Bye." I waved him away and turned toward my car.

"Ma'am," the man called out to me as I slid into the front seat of my car.

"Yes?" I rolled the window down and tossed the question over my shoulder with irritation in my voice.

"Be careful," he said and started to walk toward the elevator.

Careful would have been having a better aim at Amiri and Marissa. Instead, I was sloppy. I had no idea if any of my bullets hit their target.

Lord, help me. I caught a glimpse of Amiri stepping off the elevator, heading toward me. I had it in my mind to mow him down with my car. I tried to pull off before he reached me, but he ran over and stood behind my car, blocking my way out. My only option would be to run him over, and I was a New York minute away from doing it.

"Tess, please talk to me," he begged.

"There's no need to talk, Amiri. You should have been talking to me from the beginning. Instead, you were screwing Marissa. Please, move so that I can leave," I yelled through the cracked window.

Amiri gripped the side of the car in his hands as he walked around to the driver's door. The way he held on, had I pulled off, I would have dragged him across the parking lot.

"Baby, please hear me out," he pled.

"Don't talk to me, Amiri. Go back in there and talk to Marissa! I'm sure she and her baby will listen to you. I don't want to hear you out."

"You are the most important person in my life, Tess. You have to believe that. Please, baby," he said. "It was a mistake."

I put the car in park, flung the door open, and got out. I slapped him hard across his cheek. He caught my hand as I revved back to do it again. He brought my hand to his mouth, kissing it repeatedly. I yanked away and slapped his face with a full-throttle smack. Meaning, I used all the force in my one hundred and forty pound frame to slap the taste out of his mouth. I hit Amiri until the moment came that I would be satisfied, though I would never be satisfied.

"Amiri, how could you do this to me? I never thought you'd stoop so low as to sleep with Marissa. You played me as a fool from the beginning. So, just let me go. This is more than I can handle right now. Leave me alone before I do something else I'll regret, even worse than shooting at you and Marissa."

"Tess, you could have killed someone tonight. You need to calm down before you end up in jail."

"Amiri, spare me the self-righteous bull. You don't have to stand here and pretend to care about what happens to me. You've already shown me your true feelings."

"Listen, I feel horrible for bringing this on you like this, especially when you've been so good to me. You don't deserve this, Tess."

"You're damn right, I don't." I looked up into his hazel eyes, the ones that used to melt my whole body down to putty in his hands, just from him looking at me. "Thank goodness I didn't get pregnant by you. Now, I can make a clean break and leave you alone," I said through clenched teeth.

"Tess—"

"It would've been hard to have your baby anyway. You saved all the good sperm for Marissa." Speaking her name caused anger to rise within me. I swung at Amiri again. "I can't believe you did this to me!"

He tried to pull me into a hug, and I pushed away from his attempt to embrace me. It was far too late to hug and console one another. What we had was beyond repair.

"Okay, so you want to hear the truth? Fine, I had sex with her. It was just sex, Tess. I promise you that's all it was. I don't have feelings for her beyond that. You're the only woman I've ever loved, for real. You're the one that understands me and makes me feel whole. Please don't throw our love away. Besides, it may not even be my baby."

"Amiri, our shitty love was in the trash on our wedding night. How dare you—" I hauled off and slapped his face once again. "—fuck another woman on our wedding night?"

"Tess, I deserve every blow and so much more. Do it again," he offered his other cheek, but I didn't hit him. I just stood there looking into his eyes feeling like a wounded animal. "See, you don't want to hurt me anymore than I wanted to hurt you. I promise I'll never hurt you again, Tess," said Amiri.

He pulled me into his arms. I couldn't help but breathe in the all-powerful masculine scent that was Amiri. It assailed my senses reminding me of who he had been to me these past few years. *My husband.*

I was fire dragon hot with him, but I couldn't turn my love on and off like a switch. A blazing fire burned to my soles reminding me of the ways I loved him. On our wedding day, I pledged to love and honor Amiri forever. I cried, leaving tears all over his shirt. This hurt so bad. He trampled everything I thought was real. Our love was built on a lie. I had no other choice but to gather what was left of my life and try to fix it for my heart's sake. I pushed away from Amiri, and another smell wafted through the air.

"You know, I never thought we would be here, Amiri. Yet, here we are with you standing in my face with the scent of my best friend's pussy on your lips. You're right about one thing. You will never hurt me like this again because I won't give you the chance to."

"Tess, I'm wrong for this," he said pitifully.

"You're wrong, and I'm heartbroken and done."

"Tess—"

"It's over. I will never forgive you for cheating with Marissa. This is a double loss for me. I have no friend or husband. Thank you very much," I said as I pulled my hand away from his.

"We still have each other, Tess. It looks bad right now, but it can change...I will change," he said, grabbing my arm to pull me back to him.

"No! It's over." I yanked away from him.

"Is this man hurting you?" asked the man who tried to help me out earlier.

"We're good," Amiri replied in a husky voice.

"What's going on, then?" The man flexed his neck muscles at Amiri as he stood in front of us. Clearly over six foot tall, he was toe-to-toe with Amiri.

"Who is this, Tess?" Amiri looked at me with accusing eyes.

"Oh, that's rich, Amiri." He had some nerve to act accusatory toward me after what I had just witnessed.

The man spoke up.

"I walked by earlier and saw her crying and was worried about her. I left something in the car, came out, and saw you two arguing. Sorry to intrude," the man said. He stepped back beside his car and watched us from there.

Amiri looked at him and then me.

"Sir, I'm fine, really. I appreciate you for checking on me, but this is my husband. If anyone needs help by the end of the night, it will be him. You can trust me on that," I said, glaring at Amiri as a warning.

"Okay, Miss," the man said.

"I appreciate you stopping, though," I thanked him again.

"Anytime," the man said and stood by his car looking over at us. He didn't back down easily. He tilted his brim hat, and short, dusty brown hair escaped.

I smiled. I must say his chivalry was rare.

"The world needs more men like you," I acknowledged.

"No problem, ma'am. If you need anything...anything, especially if you ever need help getting out of jail..." The man let out a slight chuckle as he reached into his pocket and pulled out a business card. He walked back over and handed it to me. "You give me a call. The name is Jake, and my company is Rough Rider's Bail Bonding."

"Are you done with your little love connection with my wife?" Amiri cut in, glaring at Jake.

"Just being a gentleman, because, like the beautiful lady said, the world needs more of them." Jake let out an easy chuckle, then added, "With a sweet thing like that walking around, all I can say is you betta keep her eyes dry, 'cause I keep plenty of tissues."

"I'll hand you your ass, white boy," Amiri said, stepping closer to the man.

"That's cute! You want to try that out in real life?" Jake said, the muscles in his neck flexing uncontrollably.

"Fuck you," Amiri waved Jake off.

"Fuck you, too. Men like you never deserve what you have," Jake said.

Amiri's fists balled into a knot. His eyes never left Jake as Jake slid into his Corvette and sped off.

"I don't even know him, but he's right. You don't deserve me, Amiri."

"Tess…" I pointed in the direction of the elevator where Marissa was getting off. Her eyes scanned the lot. Then, she spotted us.

Amiri watched her with a guilt-ridden expression covering his handsome features. By the time he turned back to me, I was pulling out of my parking space and driving by. All hope left Amiri's eyes as we looked at each other one last time. From the daggers I shot in his direction, I let him know it was in his best interest to let my goodbye be forever. Where I was going, it would be a couple of forevers before I ever saw a human again. I was done with people.

CHAPTER THREE

Tess

It's going to take a little more time. That's what I kept telling myself as I sat in a chair by the window one month later. Alone in my parents' beachside home in Gulf Shores, I stared out at the calm blue waters cascading upon the golden sand. Soft music played from my iHome speaker. It wasn't breakup music that would make me cry over my lost love or romantic music to make me remember the good times. I listened to classical jazz and drank wine, plenty of it. It helped to keep my mood numb, almost in a state of limbo.

Have you ever felt numb? Like nothing in the world mattered? And, even if it did matter, there was nothing you cared to do about it? Well, that's exactly what I was feeling. I don't even think if someone touched me I would feel it. It was almost like dying a slow death. Shot in the heart, but still alive, living life day by day and waiting on the moment it all ends. A death from being shot in the chest and having to wait the excruciating amount of time before my lungs filled up with blood and I could no longer breathe. Except, it wasn't blood that filled my lungs. It was the loss of my parents compounded by my best friend and husband's lust for one another that filled every inch of me with despair.

I sat at the breakfast table with one arm crossed over my chest, guarding my heart. The other arm held a piping hot cup of black coffee. I stared out over the ocean and tried to feel something other than hurt. Anything.

I'd gone through a range of emotions. Sometimes wanting things to remain just as they were before I found out my husband was a cheater. I'd imagine him next to me, smiling or laughing hysterically about a joke I'd told. Or, I'd envision him making love to me while I was none the wiser to the fact that he was also in love with my best friend.

My mind mulled over the full month Amiri and I spent trying to get pregnant after we got married. How we had so much fun trying to conceive a child that would have maybe his eyes…and maybe my nose.

Then, my mind went dark. Straight to the very moment Marissa begged me not to hurt the baby growing in her stomach. The baby Amiri successfully implanted into her womb. It was dreadfully painful to hear her admittance that she was having his child…a precious child. That was the shot that hit me in the chest. The shot heard around the world, piercing my lungs and breaking my spirit. That's what had me sitting there feeling like I was suffocating while waiting on my last breath.

They say there's no honor among thieves. I guess there's no honor among friends either. The sad part was I didn't consider Marissa as only a friend. She was my sister in every sense of the word. We went to elementary school, high school, and college together. We even started an accounting business *together*. We were inseparable.

When we were in elementary, kids used to joke about my big button nose. Marissa would come through swinging, ready to beat up anyone who made jokes about me. Her bravery to stand up to those kids gave me the courage to also stand beside her. Marissa taught me to stand up for myself—only to knock my knees from under me when I least expected it.

Back then, it wasn't just Marissa defending me. I defended her too. Once, Carter McNulty told her he would rather take a chicken to the senior prom than to date her. The next day, I brought a raw chicken to school and smeared it all over his car. I left the whole chicken on his windshield with a note that read: *How about you take a real chicken to senior prom, you dickhead?*

Oh my… a smile and something close to a chuckle escaped my lips as I thought about the amount of pettiness I displayed that day in my friend's honor. I would've done anything for Marissa. That thought alone left me scratching my head and wondering why she would do this to me.

Mentally, I was exhausted from thinking about it. I traveled back in time so much trying to pin down the exact event that put my life on this downward spiral. Nothing came to mind. Trying to figure out what went wrong had my head spinning. I needed to talk to my mother.

Lord, Mom, I need you right now.

My beautiful mother, bless her warm, loving heart. She loved Marissa and treated her like she was her own. When we had a girl's day out, Marissa was right there with us. I was happy Mom wasn't alive to witness Marissa's deceitfulness. She would have been devastated over the news, almost as devastated as I was ruined.

When I left Atlanta, I drove until I reached my parents' beach home. I wanted to put as many miles as possible between me and Atlanta. I wanted to feel close to my parents. After a month in Gulf Shores, I still couldn't muster the strength to face Amiri or Marissa. Their countless calls begging for forgiveness caused me to chuck my phone out into the ocean. I didn't want to talk to anyone. All I wanted to do was sit beside the windowsill and watch days turn into nights and nights turn into days.

Before I chucked my phone, I ordered movers to go to my old house and collect my clothes and a few sentimental items my parents had given me. The rest of my things Amiri and Marissa could keep.

A knock on the door startled me from my thoughts. I wrapped my terry robe tightly around my waist and floated to the door on autopilot. When I peeked out the curtains, two handsome young men stood on the other side of the door smiling back at me. From the logo on their shirts, I knew they were the movers.

"Hello," I said after opening the door.

"Hi, I'm Lamonte from Two Men and a Truck," one of them spoke, pointing to the logo on his shirt. "I'm here with a delivery for Tess Knox. Is that you?"

"Yes, that's me. Come on in," I said and half smiled at the tall, dark and handsome young man who looked confused.

"I'm so glad we got the right place. It was really hard to find, and that's putting it lightly," he noted with a chuckle.

"I know; this isn't the easiest address to find on the GPS. I'm sorry about that," I said. "My parents intentionally bought the beach home in the cul-de-sac, surrounded by all these tall palm trees so that they could have a lot of privacy. Don't ask me why," I said, thinking of Mom and Dad and the love they shared.

The two men turned to each other and smiled.

"Well, I can see how they could get good privacy out here, but it doesn't help when someone is trying to find you," Lamonte said.

"You definitely have a point," I said and smiled as well. Though, if the truth were to be told, I wasn't trying to be found by anyone. But, it was small talk, and it felt good to smile. Human even.

"We'll unload your things and get out of your way. Just tell us where you want us to put these boxes, so you can get back to sleep," he said, still holding that polite smile.

"No, I wasn't sleeping." I chuckled, then pointed to a space in the corner of the living room. "You can put everything over here."

Lamonte walked outside to his moving van and came back in with his short and stout coworker. This man was already sweating. He smiled and spoke but let Lamonte do most of the talking.

Within thirty minutes, my boxes were off their truck and loaded into the living room. I signed off on the delivery and closed the door behind them. I looked at all the boxes. All the belongings

I had in this world didn't take up a corner in my parents' beach house. My eyes went to the ceiling.

I guess you guys knew what you were doing when you begged me not to sell this place, I said to the empty room. I had every intention to sell my parents' beloved beach home, but I remembered their urging to keep it in the family. They made me promise when they bought it that if anything ever happened to them I wouldn't sell. I was happy I followed their advice. Their home was now my home.

I huffed, preparing to sort through the boxes and put everything up. It was time to start making this place mine. I gently kicked a smaller box to the sofa and sat down. Inside, I found wash towels engraved with my first name. My mom bought those before she died. I opened another small box expecting to see more towels. Lying on top was an envelope with the words READ ME in Amiri's handwriting.

I don't need this right now. I placed the letter on the sofa beside me and continued working. Within an hour, I had unpacked and put up everything. Exhausted, I plopped down on the couch and felt a piece of paper underneath me. It was Amiri's note. Fire rose from the pits of hell and up through my soles upon seeing his handwriting. What could he possibly want?

I figured there was no time like the present to see what kind of lies he strung together. Once I read those lies, I could toss it in the trash along with our marriage. My hands trembled as I peeled back the flap and removed the thick letter. I focused on the first page and began reading.

My Dear Tess,

I don't think it's possible for me to regret anything more than I regret losing you. What this past month has taught me is that I love you to my core, but I do realize I didn't love you correctly. I made a huge mistake, and it wasn't just sleeping with Marissa that was the mistake. It was betraying the most precious gift that God ever gave to me...you, my beautiful wife. Every day that we were together, you were nothing but good to me, and I want you to know none of this reflects the magnificent woman you are. It was my selfishness that ended the best thing I ever had. You are a one of a kind woman, and you deserve better. That's why, though I do it with so much sadness and hurt, I've gone ahead and preemptively drawn and signed our divorce papers. It's not that I want to let you go, I have to, so you can be free to get what you deserve from someone who deserves your love. I never thought I'd be able to write that, much less actually go through this. But I know you don't want me back. Every day since you've been gone, I've reached out to you, even prayed you would come back, but now I've come to the conclusion that you deserve to be free of the baggage I now carry with Marissa.

Someone will honor you. I hope he comes along and loves you the way I should have. To be honest, my heart is torn right now. I'm broken because I can only imagine how alone you must feel, and I can't do anything to change that. I had no right to violate your sisterhood with Marissa. I came to your beach house in Gulf Shores four times since you left to try to tell you these things face to face. Each time, I knock and knock, and there is no answer. I know you were in there, but I can't blame you for not wanting to see me.

I haven't been with Marissa since you left. I've only been reflecting over how wrong I was...how much I love you...and what has been lost. Sorry, I didn't love you the way I vowed to do in front of God. That shortcoming will always bring me to the brink of tears, but in the end, it will strengthen me to be a better man. The kind a woman like you deserve. If you ever find it in your heart, please forgive me and then forgive Marissa. She is just as broken over this as I am.

I could go on but know this...I LOVE YOU, and I wish you the best.

Amiri

I turned the page. There were divorce papers granting me half of the proceeds of the sale of our home and half of our joint bank account. I didn't realize I was clutching onto the papers as I read over the documents until I fell back on the couch with them tight in my hands. This made everything so real, so final. Tears leaked freely from my eyes.

My perfect little world officially crashed and burned. Staying away, not answering his phone calls or opening the door for him when he came kept us apart, but yet we were still bonded by our marriage. Now, even that was over. All I needed to do was sign on the dotted line.

CHAPTER FOUR

Jake

I got to the office in time to check the court docket for the day. One of the young women I bonded out last month had court in an hour. I planned to be in court with her for her big day. After she didn't show at my office, I wasn't sure that would happen. I rechecked the time, took out my cell, and called Tiffany's number. Her voicemail picked up immediately.

"Tiff, it's approximately 8:10 a.m. I need you to meet me at the courthouse in thirty. You were supposed to be at my office now. I'm not sure what's going on, but today is important. If you don't show, you'll get a failure to appear and a warrant for your arrest. Don't call me to bail you out if that happens, okay?" I spoke firmly as if I were talking directly to her.

I wanted the best for Tiffany but held no punches back. If she didn't meet her end of her obligations, I was done dealing with her. Before I bailed Tiffany out of jail, she guaranteed me she wanted to turn her life around and would do the work to get there. She had done great so far. But her future depended on whether or not she walked into that courtroom door this morning.

When she first called me up and begged me to help her out, I was hesitant. Over the past five years as a bail bondsman, I heard stories from a lot of criminals who wanted to get out of jail free, but Tiffany's story struck a chord. She was young, fragile, and, most of all, sincere. One look into her eyes and I could see she needed someone to believe in her and to show her the way. So, I took a chance. I bonded her out without making her pay the fee.

The day after she bonded out of jail, she got a temp job, and the next week she paid part of her fee. The conditions I gave Tiffany were for her to find and keep a job and stay away from her drug dealer boyfriend, Joogie. Oh yeah and to be at my office bright and early the morning of her court hearing. She kept her word on the other things but missing this court date could land her right back at square one, losing her new job and going back to jail.

"Come on, Tiff. Do the right thing, girl," I mumbled as I picked up her file.

I wanted us to ride together, so I could give her some cues on what to say to convince the judge to drop her drug paraphernalia charge. She needed to tell the court the pipe and drugs were her ex's since they were his. It was time for her to stop taking responsibility for Joogie's criminal activity. Turning on him was something Tiffany never dreamed of doing before this arrest. She usually took whatever charge she got when the cops pulled them over, which was often since Joogie was a dunce who had no problem hanging his girl out to dry. The charges were anything from petty misdemeanors to traffic violations. Tiffany drove for him, and always took the charges…always.

She was looking at a felony for this last stop. Not only had Joogie pinned the pipe filled with drugs on her, but he also said the drugs in his trunk belonged to her. Because he stored them in one of her backpacks, his story could convince a judge.

The ball was in Tiffany's court. She had started to build a life for herself and her unborn daughter. All she had to do was show up to court and testify against her boyfriend who sold her out.

I pulled into the courthouse parking lot and felt relieved to see Tiffany standing in front of the building. I smiled as I got out of the car.

"Are you intentionally trying to stress me out?" I asked her as I walked toward her, locking my car door with my key fob.

"You didn't think I was coming, did you?" she asked, smiling as well.

Tiffany's baby bump had grown so much over the past month, and she was glowing. When I first met her, she had dark rings around her eyes, and she looked stressed to the max. Now, her eyes sparkled against the sun rays. However, underneath her glow, she looked nervous.

"I have to admit I was a little worried, but I had faith that you'd be here," I said, opening the front door of the building for us to walk inside. We got in line behind the group of people waiting to be checked by the guards.

"Thank you, Jake."

"No problem."

"Not for opening the door, for believing in me when no one else would. Not even my family believes I'm going to do the right thing. Everyone gave up on me a long time ago. They wouldn't even take my calls when I was in jail, because they think I'm a lost cause, following Joogie's every command. I'll never forget what you did for me. You believed in me, and I owe you my life. So, of course I made it to court this morning. Sorry, I didn't call you. I had some things to handle at my house before I left."

My chest swelled with pride and joy. She sounded like a young woman about to be crowned into womanhood. She was handling her business the right way.

"Everyone deserves a second chance, Tiff," I said. "You're here, and that's what matters most."

"Well, I appreciate everything you've done for me, Jake, and that's from the heart," she said.

"You're welcome. Do you want to know how you can pay me back?" I asked.

"Yes."

"By taking good care of your daughter. That's the most important thing you could do for yourself and your daughter. That would be enough for me," I told her.

Tiffany's hands shook as they dropped to her belly. She rubbed her stomach, and I knew she was thinking about the fate of her daughter.

"I promise I will. She is only the reason I decided to leave Joogie alone," she said. "But, I want you to know that no matter what happens today, you've helped me more than you could ever know."

"Don't start that whatever happens mess. *When*, not if, you walk out of here today, you'll be a free woman, and it'll be because you did the right thing by giving up your ex-boyfriend. We all have to start somewhere, and this is your first step."

Tiffany broke down in tears and started hugging me.

I returned the hug, patting her back.

We only had a little time, and I had to give her the drill of how her judge would work. Taking a step back, I began, "Listen, I've been in this judge's courtroom so many times I can repeat his opening and closing statements. What he wants is the bigger fish. He'll go lenient on you, but only if you cooperate. As long as you tell the truth and show him you've been productive since you got out on bail, you'll walk out of here a free woman today. If not scot-free from all charges, you'll get probation or community service, rehab classes or something, but you'll be walking out. Then, you'll be able to keep moving forward for your child's sake." I studied her face to see if what I was saying got through to her.

Tears ran down her cheeks.

"I hope you're right," she said, wiping her eyes.

"Do what I said, and you'll be fine, Tiff."

"Okay, Jake."

We stepped up to the guards who began their search of our belongings and scanned our body for firearms. Then, we went inside the courtroom and found a seat, hopeful about the outcome of the proceedings.

✱✱✱

"What did I tell you?" I asked her as we walked out of the courthouse two hours later. The judge had a full docket, so we had to sit through at least ten other hearings before we got to Joogie and Tiffany's case.

I had already spoken to the detectives on the case, so I knew the prosecutor wanted Joogie off the streets more than anything.

As expected, he pinned the drugs on Tiffany. When it was her turn to testify, he looked confident she would corroborate his story and send him back onto the streets a free man. Instead, Tiffany gave a compelling story about how he introduced her to drugs, and that he'd been dealing drugs since before she met him. She testified everything she knew about his operation and gave the judge and detectives specifics that would lock him up for years.

He glared at her in an attempt to intimidate her as she testified. Surprisingly, Tiffany sat there confidently. She showed no fear. She took a stand for herself and her unborn child. When we walked out of the courtroom, Joogie motioned with his hands as if he were slicing his neck—a clear threat to Tiffany. The moment she stood up for herself he tried to put fear in her.

"Threaten her again, and I will flip you like a quarter, Joogie!" I barked as I turned to walk in his direction.

One of the officers who saw him make the hand motion stepped up and started talking to him. Another officer stepped up beside me.

"Jake, we can't let you attack him in here," the officer said to me.

"Order in the court." The judge hit his gavel against his hardwood podium. "In the light of your threats against Ms. Woods, your bail is revoked," he said to Joogie.

The people supporting Joogie gasped. Others mean mugged me and Tiffany. Some made their objections known by saying how wrong the judge was. The officer next to Joogie put him in cuffs to took him to the back. Joogie smirked at Tiffany as they took him to place him in a cell.

"Come on, let's get out of here," I said to Tiffany who had nervousness covering her delicate ivory features.

"Now, I have to worry about Joogie retaliating because I know he will. He has people everywhere, and they will come for me since they put him in jail. God, what have I done? I'll never be able to live in this city again." She sighed and looked like she was about to break down at any moment.

"Tiffany, he has controlled you for so long, and now that's over. It's either suffer the consequences of taking a stand for yourself or be walked on the rest of your life. Those are the only choices. Whether you did it today or another time, you were eventually going to have to stand up for yourself."

"Yeah, that all sounds good until I have to go back to my neighborhood and deal with these people. I don't trust being in this city anymore, especially on my side of town. After today, I should be running out of town."

I thought about what she said. I had no fear of men like Joogie, but I couldn't guarantee one of his people wouldn't try to harm her. So, I was making plans in my mind to protect her.

"Go home and pack up everything you can into your car, just the essentials. Then, meet me back at my office. Better yet, I'll come with you. Get in," I said, opening my passenger door for her.

"That won't be necessary. I already packed my things into my car this morning. That's why I couldn't make it to your office. I knew I wouldn't be able to go home after this. His people were in the courtroom today, and they're probably already at my house looking for me if they're not watching us right now." She looked around the parking lot, and I scanned it looking for anything out of place.

I didn't see anything suspicious, but I agreed with Tiffany. You could never be too safe. "Follow me to my office. We'll talk about it more there. If anyone follows us there, I'll send them limping back to the other side of town," I said as I walked her to her car and opened her door.

She followed me to Rough Riders. Once there, I checked the scenery. We didn't appear to have been followed. In my office, Tiffany and I talked about a plan for her safety, at least while this mess was fresh.

"I was thinking about moving to a little town in Alabama or Tennessee. I don't know," Tiffany said. She looked lost. "I just know I can't stay in Georgia. I wouldn't feel safe."

"How about we do this for now? You go to my place and stay there until we can figure this out," I suggested.

"No, I couldn't do that, Jake. I'll figure something out. You've already done enough to help me," she said.

"No, Tiffany. You will stay with me while we work things out, and that's the plan."

This idea was foreign to me. I never mixed business with my personal life. Yet, Tiffany was worthy of someone taking a chance on her. I had talked her into doing the right thing in court. Now, I wanted her to make it. She was the kind of girl many would call white trash because she grew up in a trailer park out in Cedarwood. She left her parents' house when she started dating black guys. At twenty-two, she still hadn't made much progress in life. She spent her years since high school giving her all to men that were older than her.

"I can't let you do that for me," she said, backing away from my desk. "Like I said, you've already done so much. I'll figure this out on my own," she said and started to walk out of my office.

"Sit down," I raised my voice. The sound boomed, bouncing off the walls.

Tiffany walked back over to her chair and sat down promptly.

"Now, here're the details. I have a highly secure home. No one will get in or out unless I want them there. I have a guest bedroom and a stocked fridge," I told her. "You are welcome to anything you see in there."

"Jake, this feels too much like intruding on your personal space. I couldn't do that," she whined.

"No, you won't be intruding on me. I'm hardly home, and you can sleep in my guest bedroom. Consider yourself housesitting." I chuckled. "I'll get Lou to drive you to my apartment and stay there with you until I get home later this evening. You can leave your car parked in our garage for a while until things die down."

"Okay," Tiffany relented.

"Lou, come here for a second," I buzzed my right-hand guy.

He walked into the room with a scowl on his face. I gave him the nickname LuKane, and it wasn't because he had a generous heart. He wore a constant glower, and he was always brawling about one thing or another.

"What's up?" he asked, looking between Tiffany and me.

"Tiffany here is going stay with me until she finds a new place. Take her to my apartment and stay there with her until I get home. I should be there in a few hours."

"Sure, boss. It wasn't like I had any actual work to do today. Of course, I wouldn't mind sitting around at your condo with Tiffany," said Lou. He looked at Tiffany and did something I rarely saw him do. Smile.

"Good." I ran what happened in court down to him.

"She'll be in good hands with me," Lou said confidently.

"Thanks, Lou. I owe you one. I'll get Rico to bring her things from her car later," I said.

"Nah, boss. You don't owe me one. This makes a hundred and one if you add it to the other ones you owe me."

"You're right," I said, laughing. I could never repay Lou for having my back.

"Since I'm leaving, and Rico is probably somewhere goofing off, why don't you scan through the paper he brought in earlier to see if we can get some new business out of there?" Lou suggested. He seemed to take pride in bossing me around.

I smiled. It was a rare thing to get my partner in crime to look genuinely happy.

"I guess I will. You and Rico seem to think you're my boss and not the other way around," I scoffed.

When I started my bail bonding company four years ago, I didn't have any employees. Since then, I hired Lou and Rico who'd become family.

Lou walked out ahead of Tiffany. "Come on, Tiff. We'll go out the side door to my car," he said.

"Thanks again, Jake," Tiffany said then caught up with Lou. The grateful look in her eyes reassured me I was doing the right thing.

Once they left, I flipped through the pages of the Crime Stopper newspaper Lou gave me, scrolling through pictures of well-known petty criminals, some I bailed out before, some I didn't have any interest in dealing with again. There was Louie "Mr. Five Finger Discount" smiling as if he'd just hit the lottery and Tammy "The Notorious Car Jacker Helper" crying as if she had no idea stealing cars was a crime.

Almost at the end of the list, an exclusive column asking for information on the whereabouts of a woman who discharged a firearm at Lexington Enterprises caught my eye. I hauled the paper closer to my face to get a good look at the most angelic person I'd ever seen.

"What the hell?" I said as I looked over the charges against her.

Listed amongst two-bit criminals of Atlanta was the woman I encountered last month in Lexington Enterprises' car garage. She ran out of the building arguing with her husband about his affair. I was amazed to see that she was wanted for the unlawful firing of a firearm inside an occupied building. Lexington Corporation had camera footage of her shooting and offered a reward for her whereabouts.

"Why don't they just bring in the bastard husband of hers?" I mumbled.

Anger rose inside of me. I couldn't explain the feeling. I should have broken her husband's nose when I had the chance. He made this gorgeous woman look sleazy in the Crime Stopper paper when he was one that had his hands dirty. The article stated she left town, and her husband had no idea where she went. *Pitiful.* He couldn't protect his woman's heart, so of course he couldn't keep up with her. The hurt in her eyes that night flashed in my mind. That look haunted me for days after I first saw her. Now, that feeling was back. I had to find her and do what I could to help her out of this mess.

CHAPTER FIVE

Tess

At sunset, I sat in front of the window watching the sun dim and seemingly drop into the ocean. I thought of Amiri's letter and the divorce papers. I had yet gotten the nerve to sign them. Days had passed, and they sat in the middle of the kitchen table like a centerpiece, alone and untouched. Ever so often I'd pick them up, read over every agonizing word, then gently slide the papers back to the middle of the table. A knock at the door startled me from going through that routine again. As I walked to the front door, a rush of hope washed over me.

Amiri. He must've known I read his letter. Maybe he had come to talk things over. A smile settled on my lips as my steps quickened. I didn't know why, but, at that moment, I craved to see him. I missed my husband deeply.

A few steps away from the door, precaution halted my footsteps. What would I say when I saw him? Would I fall back into his arms and spend the night with him pretending he never ripped my heart out? Would I slap him and go ballistic again?

More sturdy knocks made me ask, "Who is it?"

I pushed back the curtains to look outside. It wasn't Amiri on the other side of the door. It was a tall, white man dressed in jeans and a t-shirt, and I had no earthly idea why he was there. *He must be at the wrong house,* I thought.

"Can I help you?" I asked.

"I'm Jake from Rough Riders. I need to speak with you, ma'am."

"What do you want?" I asked.

"Are you Tess Knox?"

Fear raked through every fiber of my body when he said my name. He was at the right house, but who was he?

"Yes, I'm Tess, but I don't know anything about Rough Riders. What do you want?"

"I need to talk to you about a serious matter, ma'am."

He was starting to spook me out with his vague answers.

"I'm not going to open my door to a complete stranger, so you will have to tell me why you are here first," I said, anxiously staring at the blue curtain.

"Tess, just let me in so we can—"

"I'm not opening this door. What I'm about to do is call the police." I took a step away from the door, knowing full well I didn't have a way to call anyone. I tossed my cell into the ocean weeks ago.

Damn you, Amiri. It was his fault I was here and his fault that I threw my phone into the ocean. All because of Amiri, I had to deal with this stranger on my own. Where's a good can of mace when you need it?

"There's no need for calling the police, Mrs. Knox."

"Wait a minute," I said softly, as the name Rough Riders and his voice started to resonate. *He can't be the guy from*

*Atlanta...*I tossed the thought out of my mind as quickly as it came.

Then, he said, "I'm here because the police are looking for you for shooting up your husband's office in Atlanta. I'd like to tell you how I can help."

I gasped, flinging the door open to look eye to eye with Jake.

CHAPTER SIX

Jake

Tess flung the door open with a frown on her face. I tried to hold my composure upon seeing her, but my, my, my, the mocha brown covering her gorgeous oval face spoke to me like Adele's song, *Hello*. Even with the frustrated scowl wrinkling her tender features, she was stunningly beautiful.

The very first day I saw her beautiful mocha self in that parking garage, crying over her husband, I fell for her unusually fast and hard. It wasn't the "oh, she's hot" type of fall, but the "I think I would move mountains for one taste from her lips" type of fall. I wanted to be her hero from that very moment. My brain held my body at bay the first night I met her when all I wanted to do was demolish her husband, take her into my arms, and keep her there as I wiped her tears away. I couldn't do that. She had a man, even though he was bullshitting her in the middle of a hot, muggy parking lot. I knew he was full of it from the way he desperately tried to explain away his cheating. Still, it was a personal matter. Who was I to intervene?

That was then.

After reading the full story about how she shot at him and his mistress and the charges she was up against, I felt compelled to offer my help. Her lousy predicament gave me a unique opportunity to get close to her. No, I wasn't her bondsman, and there wasn't a bounty on her. I set out to find Tess to help her clear her name. And, there I was, staring into her perfect, dark, doe eyes.

Tess seemed gentle, like a rose. A regal, virtuous woman who had been mishandled. Hiding my feelings for her was going to be hard, maybe even impossible now that I stared down into her pretty brown eyes. My eyes drifted to her perky breasts peeking out of the royal blue terry robe.

"Heeellllloooo!" she said, bringing my attention from her body to the reason I was there. "What do you mean the police are looking for me?" she asked with an attitude. She was still adorable and that made me smile.

"Do you mind if I call you Tess?" I asked.

"Call me whatever you want. I don't care. Just please explain why the police want me," she said. Her eyes slanted into a look of disbelief as if it never occurred to her shooting up a corporate building would come back to haunt her. The reservations building in her eyes were somehow irresistibly sexy.

"Are you going to invite me in, or do we have to talk about it in the doorway?" I asked as I studied the contours of her flawlessly sculpted oval face. God showed favor when he created her inside of her mother's womb. She was somewhere between Tyra Banks beautiful and Beyoncé fine, and that was just her physical beauty.

I could have sent Lou or Rico to bring her back to me. I came personally because I wanted the honor of tracking her. She seemed to have fallen off the side of the earth until I traced her movers to Alabama. As she stood in front of me chock-full of fire, the only thing I could think of was how badly I wanted to keep her for myself.

"None of this is making sense," she said, still guarding the doorway.

I appreciated her carefulness. I cursed the day anyone harmed a hair on her head. I would never forget the day I looked into her pain-filled eyes and wished I could be the one responsible for turning her hurtful tears into joyful ones. I never wanted to make a woman happy as much as I wanted to at that moment. The feeling was baffling.

"It's simple. The police are looking for you for the gunshots at your husband's office, and that's also why I'm here. I'll explain what's going on, but I didn't drive a whole state over just to stand outside," I said.

Finally, she stepped aside to allow me in.

"How do you know they're looking for me? And, how do I know I can trust you?" she asked.

"How have you been?" I couldn't help but ask.

"Just fine until you got here. Now, tell me what's going on."

"I didn't want us to meet again under these circumstances," I explained.

She gasped and covered her mouth. "Gosh, you really are the guy from the parking lot that night. I took your card. You're a bounty hunter or something like that, right?"

"Bail bondsman and bounty hunter, yes, that's what I do."

She glared at me as if she wanted to toss me back out the door.

"Are you here to take me to jail?" she asked. "Oh, my god. You're taking me to jail," she panicked.

Watching her beautiful features scrunch up into a horrified frown did something to me. I had to put her mind at ease.

"No, Tess, I'm not taking you to jail. I'm not going to candy coat this for you either. You have some pretty tough accusations against you. One is for shooting at Marissa Thompson, which carries a reckless endangerment charge, and you know she's pregnant, right?"

She narrowed her eyes at me.

"Yeah, of course, I know my best friend is carrying my husband's baby. You ever stop to think that maybe that's the reason I shot at her?" she seethed.

"Look, I'm not trying to take a dig. I want you to recognize the extent of what you're dealing with legally. The second accusation is the destruction of property for the bullets that hit the walls," I said.

"Who ratted me out to the police? I bet it was Marissa. Everything is all about her these days," she said.

"No, it was one of the security guards who heard the gunshots. He called the police that night."

I took the paper out of my jacket pocket and turned to the page her story was on, then handed it to her. She quietly read the article. When she finished, she tossed the paper down on the table and rolled her eyes.

"I don't see what the big deal is. It's not like any of the bullets hit their target."

I chuckled.

"You're lucky none of your bullets hit anyone, but even though they didn't, this is still a serious matter. The district attorney is siding with the CEO of Lexington who wants to press charges. And, you have a warrant for your arrest. That's where I come in."

"I swear, I'm sick of all of this," she yelled. "I don't care. Take me to jail, but at least let me put on some clothes first." Her eyes seemed to grow bigger with the shock of her statement. "My God, I can't go to jail!" she screamed.

While she panicked about jail, something else had my attention. The mention of her needing to put on clothes caused my eyes to roam over her light brown legs, which shined to perfection. They looked smooth as honey, and the last thing I wanted her to do was to cover them.

"Calm down. You're not going to jail, Tess."

"Go ahead. Do what you have to do..." She held her wrists out to me in surrender before what I said registered in her mind.

If only I were there under different circumstances, I would take her up on her offer to cuff her.

CHAPTER SEVEN

Tess

I held my hands out to him. I surrendered to be handcuffed and carted off to Atlanta to be jailed like a hardened criminal. When Jake's arms stayed folded across his buff chest, my eyes collided with his to see what was taking him so long to move. A hint of something mysterious bedazzled me as his eyes traveled to my breasts and down to my legs. That's when what he said hit me.

"What do you mean? I thought that's why you were here."

"For the thousandth time, I'm not here to take you to jail. You don't have to get dressed or handcuffed. I come in peace. I'm only here to help."

I cleared my throat to get his attention away from my legs. With the brooding look on his face, a blind woman could see underneath his charming, chivalrous ways. He was a lady killer. Warm, gray eyes were a cover-up for the fact that his very essence could penetrate hearts and desecrate souls. I stopped looking into his eyes when a feeling I didn't recognize tingled inside my gut. This man was trouble in every way known to woman. His gray gaze roamed over mine, and I just knew he could see how damaged I was. What better time to prey on a woman than when she's already in distress? I didn't need anything else to pile on. Jake needed to make his intentions clear at once.

"How are you going to help me?" I asked.

"It's messed up what your husband did to you," he began. "That's why I'm going to pull some strings at the police department to see if I can help you get out of this trouble," he said in a sincere tone.

I looked away from his intense gaze.

"Why would you do that for me? You don't know me," I asked.

"Because I don't like what he did to you," Jake said matter-of-factly.

Waves of nervousness fluttered in my gut.

"But what's it to you? What makes you care about what happens to me?"

"To be honest, from the very first time I saw you, I was drawn to you. It was meant for me to be in that car garage at the time that I was. You needed protection, and I was placed there to give it to you. Though you wouldn't let me help you then, I have another chance now. That's why I'm here."

"Maybe I won't give you a chance this time either," I said, still trying to decide if I wanted to trust his motive for showing up in Alabama.

"Tess, that night could have ended tragically, but it didn't. A blind man can see that you're not a bad person. None of your actions that night are who you are. You don't have a record, and you've never been in any kind of trouble. I did my research and found out that you actually are quite the woman. You help other people and work with charities that serve the community. you

shouldn't get time for something you did out of pure emotion."
Jake's heavy southern drawl filled the room with baritone
dominance as he spoke.

I rode the wave of each decibel. It wasn't until he stopped
talking that I noticed the vibrations resonated. There's no way I
should've felt tingles run down my spine when I looked at Jake,
but it was the result of going too long without human contact.

"Thank you for saying those things, Jake. But, just out of
curiosity, how do you research me?" I asked.

"I looked you up on social media and asked around. You
are a giver. You care about people. You are not a deranged shooter
who hurls bullets around for sport," Jake acknowledged.

"I'm glad someone recognizes I'm not a horrible person.
Seems all the people who were supposed to know that have run all
over me," I said, thinking about the two beloved people I spent
years of my life cherishing.

"It's the way this world turns, Tess."

"I think it's ironic that the first time we met I didn't want
your help. Now, I need it," I said, eager to accept any help that
would keep me from seeing the inside of a jail cell.

It was ironic that Amiri and Marissa broke my heart,
leaving me to depend on a stranger for help. At one point, it was
Amiri I needed to breathe. I would inhale air into my lungs, and he
would exhale my breaths. Living without Amiri had been
suffocating. When the divorce papers arrived, I hated the thought
of our marriage ending. The finality froze me. I wanted it to be
over, yet I still hadn't broken free from him. I couldn't breathe

without him. That's how this 'til death do us part' thing works, right? Love and commitment until the very end? Well, that's what it meant for me. When I recited my vows to Amiri, I said those words with everything in me. It was hard to just bury my feelings, even when faced with the blatant deceit.

I was wanted in Atlanta for shooting at my husband and ex-bestie. If I hadn't seen it in the paper with my own eyes, I wouldn't believe it. Having a man standing in the middle of my house telling me he could help me stay out of jail solidified the fact that I was a fugitive of my love for Amiri. I didn't even want to think of Marissa's part in all of this. I could only lament one betrayal at a time. I looked back at Jake whose lips were moving.

"Sorry, what were you saying?" I asked.

He raised a brow. "What's on your mind?"

"A lot," I said. "My biggest concern is my legal problems."

"May I sit down, so we can talk?" Jake asked.

"Sure, yes," I pointed toward the living room.

Jake took the love seat, while I sat across from him on the couch. His eyes roamed all over me, looking me up and down. Jake did nothing to hide the wrinkle in his forehead that showed his appreciation of what he saw.

"Tess, we both know you're not the type of woman whose name should be displayed in the Crime Stopper's newspaper. That spot should be reserved for the real criminals of Atlanta," he said.

Though I would have had no problem if one of my bullets had hit Amiri in his backside, I said, "I should never have gotten myself into this position."

"That's why I'm here," Jake said. "When I saw law enforcement was looking for you, I had to do something." Jake leaned back on the seat, making himself comfortable.

Looking at him stretch out made me fully aware of his dominating physical presence. I suddenly felt as if I should definitely be wearing more clothes. I pulled at the corners of my robe.

"If you accept my help, I'll get you a meeting with the DA and the CEO at Lexington. Are you willing to talk to them?" he asked.

"I don't think I'm in a position to turn down your help or a meeting with the DA. I'll talk to whoever. I don't want to go to jail."

"Good." Jake's piercing gaze wandered over my face. "Can I tell you something?"

"Sure."

"That night in the parking lot, I wanted to take you away from whatever was hurting you, but you kept telling me you were fine. I didn't want to cause more trouble for you," he admitted.

Memories of gunshots ringing out, hot tears running down my cheeks, and losing people I loved to betrayal and lust rattled my soul. I envisioned prison bars closing in front of me and spending my life in a cell. Then, the panting began. I gasped for air.

"Can we not talk about that night right now? That was the worst day of my life. I don't want to be labeled a criminal, and God knows I don't belong in jail."

Feeling a burning sensation in my chest, it felt as though my lungs were on fire and would shut down at any moment. With my chest rising and falling erratically, pants raked through me. No matter how many breaths I took, it seemed like I couldn't catch a good breath. The next thing I knew, Jake's arms were all around me.

"It will be alright, Tess. You will make it through this," he said, comforting me.

"I can't—"

I wanted to tell him I couldn't breathe, but the words wouldn't come out. Jake eased me out of the chair and into his arms completely. He rubbed my back slowly.

"You're going to make it through this, Tess," he repeated, his lips pressed against my ear.

I tried to step out of his arms, but he pulled me back into them and continued to rub my back.

"Just let it all out. Don't hold it inside of you," he said.

Jake spoke to me as if he knew me. He held me tight as tears rolled down my cheeks. My warm tears covered his shirt.

"I'm sorry for wetting your shirt," I whispered as I wiped the tears away.

"I don't care about that," he assured me as he held me in his arms.

"He treated me like I was the only one he could ever love. He gave me the world and made me feel like I was on top of it. Everyone thought we were perfect, and I did too. Seeing them together toppled the castle he built on the hill for me. Now, I'm just stuck in limbo, trying to figure out who the hell I am and what is my life," I confessed my heartbreak to Jake. I don't know why, but I felt comfortable enough to open up to him.

"You'll get through this, and you'll find someone who will treat you the way you deserve to be treated."

I pushed out of his arms and paced the room with my arms crossed over my chest. "You don't know what it feels like to have your heart snatched out of your chest. You don't know what it's like to play the fool on your wedding night. They're laughing at me. Everyone probably is," I argued.

"You're right. I don't know what it feels like to play the fool on my wedding night. But—"

I interrupted, "On top of everything, I lost my parents only a few years ago, which leaves me alone in this shitty world with shitty people who only use or deceive me."

"Not all people are shitty, Tess."

I stopped walking the floor to look at Jake.

"You don't count. You're here to take me to jail."

"Well, not actually, but you're right... I don't count," he said with a hint of sarcasm in his voice.

"I didn't mean it that way. You know what? Forget it," I said.

I felt myself becoming short of breath, and once again, Jake's arms surrounded me.

"You are going to make it through this, Tess," he said.

As he held me, I gasped for air until my breathing returned to normal. Jake's essence wrapped around me like a blanket. I laid my head on his shoulder and slowly gave in to the relaxing feeling of being held. When Jake took a deep breath in, I took one out. Human connection. I missed it and apparently needed it. It had nothing to do with him being a handsome man. Absolutely nothing. At least, that's what I repeatedly told myself.

"Thank you." I stepped out of his arms, once again breaking free of his hold.

"I didn't come here to upset you. I just wanted—" he paused and looked at me. "—honestly...to see you again."

I chuckled lightheartedly. "You didn't have to travel this far to see me. I'll be behind bars in Georgia soon. Anyone who wants to see me can visit the county jail."

"I'm going to be honest with you. You have a legal battle waiting for you back in Atlanta, but you will win your case without spending one night in jail, Tess," he said.

My name and jail in the same sentence had my heart thumping against my chest.

"I sure hope you're right, Jake. Should I get ready to go back to Atlanta now to speak to the police?" I asked, ready to ride back to the city I left behind.

"No, stay put for a few days. I'll work some things out on my end so that when you return the DA will be ready to meet with you, and we can get this thing buried." Jake sounded so confident that it gave me hope. The man looked like he could fix every trouble in the world.

I smiled. "Thank you, Jake."

His gray eyes glazed over with darkness as they had earlier when they roamed my body devouring it like a gourmet meal.

"Tess, you're going through a lot, and I know you feel alone. I grew up in a foster home with people who could care less if I made it back home each day after school or if I turned into roadkill."

"Oh, Jake."

"No, I didn't tell you that for pity. I just wanted to let you know that I know how it feels to have your world turned upside down. It's a tough road, but strong people get through tough things. Trust me on that," Jake assured.

"Life gives us so many things to overcome. Sometimes, no one is who they seem. I've been crying for over a month, and I feel too weak to deal with it all."

"Listen, you shot up a place. You're not weak at all."

We both laughed.

"Not like that, Jake. You know what I mean."

"I do, but crying doesn't mean you're weak. It means you're still alive and you give a damn. It means you're not afraid to express how you feel," he said.

"A man with a sensitive side. It's rare these days," I said, smiling.

"Listen, I've had a shitload of setbacks in my life. My mother gave me up for adoption because she couldn't deal with the rejection of my father. Once he found out she was pregnant, he split on us. She was his young plaything, and he was a rich billionaire who enjoyed the fun and games until she got pregnant.

The day she came to his place of business and told him she was two months pregnant was the day he let his staff know she wasn't allowed back on the premises."

"Wow, that's terrible."

"At twenty, my mother was devastated. Imagine having been courted by a rich and famous man, given expensive gifts, and treated to his vacation homes, only to find out the product of those rendezvous, your unborn child, is the reason he kicked you out of his life," Jake said.

"I would be pissed. I would have probably killed the man," I said.

"I believe you would." Jake laughed. "But, that's my father for you. My mother isn't much better. She didn't want me. She wanted him. So, yeah. I know a little about feeling rejected by those who should've loved me. I also know how to overcome anything that makes me feel weak. Life is full of shitstorms and shitty people. The question is, how are we going to deal with them? Are we going to get an umbrella and walk through the rain, or are you going to get drenched, catch pneumonia, and die?"

"Well, that's one way to think about it. When I think about the way your parents treated you, it makes my problems seem so small. You're a good man to have been through that and to be as strong as you are."

"That's life. As bad as my situation was with my foster families, some people had it worse than me. Children were sexually abused and beaten. There's always someone with a story that will make you feel like your life isn't so bad after all. I'm not saying your pain isn't legitimate, because it is. I'm just saying, you can and will get through it. If I have anything to do with it, you will be over it in no time."

"Well..." I paused and looked into his eyes. "Thank you."

"No thanks necessary."

"Jake, it just feels like every day it's a constant struggle. I guess it doesn't help that I've isolated myself to this house. At first, it made me feel closer to my parents, but as the days go by, I'm starting to feel lost without them being here with me."

"Maybe you could use different scenery."

"Yeah, I wish I could go to Wakanda or some other fairytale land and disappear from it all," I joked.

With that, we shared another laugh. It was the most heartwarming thing to see his cheeks dimple to perfection. I had no doubt he was a heartbreaker down to his very core. I kept that in mind as I dealt with him. All men would be at arm's length as far as I was concerned.

"I can't help you get to fairytale land, but how about you spend a few days at the resort I checked into? It's a beautiful place."

"Sounds tempting, but I'll just stay here," I said.

"At least, let me take you to lunch to discuss your case," he suggested.

"That I can do," I said and smiled.

CHAPTER EIGHT

Jake

I didn't think this all the way through. All I wanted was to see her again. Now that I accomplished that feat, all I wanted to do was get her in my bed. I know I should be ashamed for thinking of sex when she was dealing with so much other drama, but damn, Tess was the most beautiful and sexually appealing woman I had ever seen. The way she stood there with pouty lips and troubled eyes made me want to gather her up in my arms, pin her against the wall, and pound her hurt away. My body was on fire at just the thought of being in the same city as Tess, much less the same room.

It didn't help that I hadn't been with a woman since my ex-girlfriend, Julie, lost her everlasting mind and tried to set my car on fire a month ago. It was the day after I first laid eyes on Tess. I didn't go home that night. Instead, I hung out at the bar with Lou until about four in the morning. Julie swore I was out sleeping with another woman. She threw a tantrum, and I put her out of my condo. I thought the crazy woman had gone home when she slammed my door. Instead, she was outside trying to brutalize my car. I never really figured she was the marrying type, but for her to trash my car was a no-go. Julie had a mean streak out of this world, but I did enjoy my time with her.

Leaving Tess all alone in that beach house reminded me of everything I'd been missing. I stood outside her door, with my manhood threatening to burst out the fabric of my pants. I readjusted it to a better position, so that hopefully the swelling would subside. I took a deep breath and walked to my car.

Once inside, I drove back to the hotel and went to my room. I flung myself onto my bed and thought about Tess. At first, I believed she recognized my attraction to her. Then, I realized she thought I was the enemy too. I would definitely change that.

My phone vibrated in my pocket, alerting me to messages Tiffany and Lou sent while I was with Tess. That's another thing about Tess. In her presence, I dared to check my phone. I gave my attention to her undivided. I would always be in tune with her that way.

But why? Why was I feeling like that about a woman I just met? I didn't feel that way about Julie, which ended up being the reason she tried to demolish the one thing she knew I loved. My Corvette. I got incensed again thinking about Julie trying to damage my baby who's never done a thing to anyone except get me where I needed to go in style.

Perhaps, I couldn't commit to Julie because I still had oats to sew. If that was true, I couldn't explain the way I felt about Tess. She made me feel like risking it all and settling down. I never wanted to be anyone's protector as badly as I wanted to protect her. I helped people out all the time, like Tiffany, but not based on attraction. Nothing fiery down in the pit of my soul burned for another as it burned for Tess. *Man, I'm gone, and I haven't even kissed the woman.*

The way I felt sounded like it belonged in a romance novel, not in my head. I looked down at my dick, and my pants were tented. The mere thought of her brought my body alive. This woman would be the death of me. That much I knew.

My phone buzzed again. That time, it was Lou calling instead of texting.

"It's Jake. What's up?" I answered.

"Bout damn time you answer the phone. I've been trying to call you all day. The office could have been blown to smithereens by now, and you'd just be answering the phone. That's not cool, boss man."

"But, the office is not blown to smithereens. You're talking to me now, so shoot," I replied.

"I'm just calling to let you know I'll be staying here with Tiff tonight so that she feels safe, and to be sure no one tries anything. She was pretty shaken up earlier. I didn't want to leave her alone," my second in command said. With Lou on the job, Tiffany had no reason to worry.

"Okay, ...sounds like a good plan. What is she doing now?"

"Hey, Jake!" I heard Tiffany's voice beam onto the line.

"Do you have me on speaker?" I asked Lou.

"Yeah man, Tiff and I were sitting here watching TV. We both wanted to call and check on you and let you know the game plan for tonight."

"Yeah Jake, everything's good. Did you make it to Alabama safely?" Tiffany asked in a bubbly tone.

I quirked a brow. Those two sounded rather cozy together.

"Yeah, I'm here. Get me off the speaker, Lou!" I said.

"Okay man, you're off now. What's up?"

"You better make sure you two don't end up in my bed, while you're over there sounding all lovey-dovey on each other," I warned Lou.

"No bro, it's nothing like that. Just keeping the lady entertained and making sure she's safe, that's all." Lou sounded mischievous even as he said that. He never kept his hands to himself. I made myself a mental note to talk to him about Tiffany. He was a twenty-six-year-old womanizer, and she had gone through enough already. She didn't need any new players in her life.

"I hear you man, but I'm serious about my bed. You sleep on the couch. Stay out of my guest bedroom too."

"I'm already set up in your room right now," Lou teased.

"You're looking to get hurt, I see."

"We're not getting in your bed, Mr. Jake, and he's not coming into the guest bedroom with me. I promise you that," Tiffany chimed in the background.

"You might as well put the phone on speaker since she knows what I'm saying anyway," I said to Lou.

"Hey, don't blame me, boss man. The girl has supersonic ears. I'll just put us back on speaker," Lou said while laughing.

"I wasn't trying to eavesdrop; I just know what's going on," Tiffany said.

"Uh huh." I yawned. "I'm glad you guys called to check on me. You haven't heard from any of Joogie's people, have you?"

"No, I haven't heard from anyone personally, except a few family members called and said Syonne is looking for me. He made a post on social media about snitches needing stitches," said Tiffany.

Syonne was Joogie's right hand in the streets. I had some things in the works with the police department to get him off the streets soon.

"Okay. I want you to stay off social media, and don't worry about anything they're saying on there. You're safe where you are."

"Don't worry. I'll take good care of her," Lou said, butting in. "If any woman, man or child comes this way looking to hurt Tiffany, they're going to find a major problem."

"Good to hear, man. You two have a good night," I said, before hanging up. I fell back on the bed thinking about Tiffany's situation.

Joogie's people were always on a retaliation mission against people who told the truth about their operation. Syonne was going to have to be dealt with. I texted the detective I worked with at the police department and waited to hear back from him. Meanwhile, it sounded like Lou would be more than happy to annihilate anyone that came near Tiffany. What I heard in his voice reminded me of the way I felt about protecting Tess. She was mine to protect, and she didn't even know it yet.

CHAPTER NINE

Tess

After Jake left, I walked around the quiet house thinking about my parents and the trouble I caused for myself in Atlanta. I thought about it so long that my nerves were on end. I walked over to the sliding glass door and looked out at the ocean. It was the spot in the house I went to feel connected with my parents.

"Mom, why did you have to leave me? Dad, I need to hear your voice right now. You two left me here, knowing you were all I had!" I screamed, and a deep pain shot through my stomach at the thought of never seeing my parents again. People said the pain would get easier with time, but, every time I thought about them, my heart ached as much as it did the day they died.

I was too nervous to cry and in too much emotional turmoil not to cry. I didn't know what to do with myself, so I jumped up and started packing. I had to get out of that house. I'd been cooped up for too many days. My mind wouldn't stop racing through scenarios of the bad things that would happen to me.

Before I knew anything, I was fully dressed, in my car, and pulling into the parking lot of the resort Jake suggested to me. I tossed my overnight bag over my shoulder and got out the car. Walking through the lobby, I looked around the beautifully designed building and observed the upbeat décor. I inhaled a deep breath. It felt good to be out and about, for a change.

After I checked into a room, I took a long, hot shower. When I finished, I dabbed on some Majesty perfume and slipped into a cute nightgown. I rubbed on the fragrance and put on the gown, hoping beautiful things would make me feel better, and it worked. I didn't feel back to normal, but it was a different feeling than I had over the past month.

I teased my hair and gave it some body, then pranced around in the mirror allowing myself to feel gorgeous for a moment. Seeing my old glow made me smile. There she was staring back at me. Tess. The girl who grew up believing she was a true-life princess because her father said so.

You are the most beautiful girl to ever live on this earth...next to your momma, you know? My father would spit out a line about how pretty I was at the drop of a dime. Each time, I soaked up every word. My father's presence surrounded me as I thought about him.

"Daddy, why did Amiri cheat on me, if I'm so beautiful?" the question spilled out of my lips before I knew it.

My sweet daughter, some men don't know how to treat the best things they have. It doesn't mean that thing isn't great. It just means they're too stupid to understand how to treat it.

My father's voice boomed against the walls as clear as day. The smell of his brand of cologne, Isimiaki, enraptured me.

"I miss you so much, Daddy."

I wrapped my arms around my chest and hugged myself for the longest time. I could feel him inside the embrace.

I miss you too, my sweet daughter. I love you more than you will ever know.

A tear rushed down my cheek.

"I love you too, Daddy. Why can't you just come back?"

Because baby, my time is up. I taught you everything you need to know to survive what you're going through. You have to walk on your own. I have to go back and be with your momma. My father's voice cracked when he said he had to leave.

"Dad, tell Momma, I said hello and that I miss her," I said, still embracing myself.

I will tell her, but please know she loves and misses you too. Be strong, my beautiful daughter.

For a few more moments, I could sense my father's essence lingering in the room. Then, he was gone.

I sat staring at the wall until exhaustion engulfed me. I climbed into bed and looked around the beautifully decorated, cream-colored room. I laid my head on the plush pillow and was fast asleep within seconds.

***

The next morning, I awakened and dressed. Sitting in front of my vanity again, I added the finishing touches to my hair. I chose to wear it in an upswept curly do with spirals of curls hanging loose to encase my face. I didn't know why, but I felt like making my outside look spunky, which was the opposite of what I felt inside. I chose a red romper that fit my curves like a glove. A month of eating light had me looking and feeling like a supermodel.

It had been a while since I felt gorgeous, but that's how I felt as I made my way to the breakfast lounge with a little pep in my step. I placed my order, sat down, and pulled out the new cell phone I purchased that morning. I started programming the phone as I waited for my food. When a set of massively large hands gripped my shoulders, I tensed to the touch. Then, Jake's voice sent ripples of calm down my spine.

"Now, this is what I call a pleasant surprise," he said.

"Oh hey, good morning," I said, turning to look into his strikingly gorgeous gray eyes. "I took your advice and came out of that stuffy house. I'm glad you suggested this place. It's kind of nice."

"I'm glad you like it, and gladder that you came here. There's not a lovelier sight than coming down and seeing you sitting here. This has made my morning."

"Oh, stop it." I blushed.

"No, really. I hope you don't mind me saying that you look amazing, today," he said as he stood his divinely built frame in front of the chair across from me.

I felt something inside of me shift. Giddiness took over me, and I wasn't the giddy type. Physically, it was hard not to be attracted to a man with a swagger such as Jake's. He was also fine as wine.

"Thanks for the compliments. You don't look bad yourself this morning," I countered.

"Do you mind?" he asked, pointing to the chair in front of him.

I motioned for him to sit down. "Of course not. Please sit down and eat with me. I hate eating alone."

Jake wore an all-black ensemble—black tee, black jeans, and black tennis shoes. He looked like he had something to hide or possibly wanted to hide in plain sight. He looked stealthy, almost sneaky. *What am I thinking? All men are sneaky.*

Rage ignited and burned through me like wildfire as I thought about the sneaky betrayal that hadn't left my mind in the past month. Ever since I saw Amiri and Marissa together, the thought of his tongue sliding dangerously close to her womanhood seconds before I caught them replayed in my mind repeatedly. I hated that those thoughts kept my mind engrossed with rage, but it was the perfect repellant to fight off my attraction to Jake. It was a reminder that I didn't want or need another broken heart. No thanks to another steel blade of a cold knife twisted into my back.

He's probably just like Amiri.

Drop dead gorgeous. Check.

Tall and dangerously sexy. Check.

A woman magnet. Check.

A best friend fucker. More than likely, check.

Though I don't have any best friends left to screw. So uncheck.

Unaware of the wave of cynicism sweeping through me, Jake smiled and began looking at his menu.

"What are you thinking about?" he asked a few minutes later. Jake stared at me with so many questions in his gray eyes.

"Nothing," I replied, pursing my lips tightly.

"If you're around me long enough, you will trust me enough to open up to me. I'm easy to talk to, and your secrets are safe with me," Jake said.

"I don't see why I need to open up. I'm wide open right now. You picked me out of a lineup in a crime newspaper. As you can see, my life is an open book." I laughed sheepishly.

"Tess, I don't think of you like that. I—"

"Hey, Jake! Long time no see," an equally built and sexy man interrupted Jake before he could finish his sentence.

"Hey Frank," Jake stood and greeted him. "What the hell have you been up to?"

"Not much. I moved to Alabama years ago, and I love it here. When I saw you from the bar, I kept looking; then, I said that's gotta be Jake. How are you doing, you bastard?" Frank extended his hand in greeting. When Jake reached to take his hand, he pulled Jake into a brotherly hug. The men battled for dominance in their embrace but were equally matched.

I was glad that Frank's interruption came right in time to deflect from the conversation Jake had initiated.

"Is this the wife?" Frank asked.

"No, but someone I'm trying to get to know better," Jake answered and turned to wink at me. "Tess, this is my good old friend, Frank Laurels, from my childhood, and we went to the academy together."

"Hi, how are you?" I asked.

"Fine, nice meeting you," said Frank. "Don't let this guy give you a hard time. He's known for it," Frank added then pretend punched Jake on the shoulder.

"I would give anyone a hard time, but her," Jake said, winking at me again.

I smiled and turned my attention back to my phone while they talked.

Jake would look at me and smile periodically.

"I guess I need to get out of the way and let you two get back to your date. It was good seeing you, buddy. Here's my number for you to call me while you're here. We must link up and hang out sometime," said Frank.

"Yes, we'll have to do that, man," said Jake.

"Also, if you want to double date, I'll snag a babysitter and bring the wife. She needs to hang out more. All she's been doing is tending to our new baby girl, and it's stressing her out. What do you say, Tess? A double date?" Frank asked me.

I humped my shoulders and answered out of courtesy. "Sure, yeah."

Jake smiled and agreed. "Good idea, man. We'll do that," he said. "But a kid, man? You settled down and became a dad? I would never have imagined it. That's wild to even say in the same sentence. Now, I know we need to catch up."

"Sure thing. Yep, we have a lot to catch up on. Fatherhood is kicking my butt, man."

"Congratulations, Frank. I know you're great dad."

"Thanks, Jake. Just let me know the time, and we'll set something up to hang out again," Frank said with a chuckle then walked away.

I smiled, seeing how happy Jake was talking to his friend. That's how friendship was supposed to be. Not dirty and foul, losing its luster on desktops.

"How long has it been since you guys have seen each other?" I asked.

"Let's see; it's been about four years. And, that's odd for us because we grew up very close. As soon as we graduated high school, we went to the police academy. Then, he realized being a cop wasn't for him. The Atlanta PD was too corrupt. There was always a new scandal going on in narcotics, so he quit, saved enough cash to leave Atlanta and got the hell out of dodge. I guess this is where he ended up. Me, I left the force not long after he did. I preferred to advocate for the people who were convicted that got a bad shake than the officers who wrongfully arrested them."

"Wow! You're a good man."

"To some people, yeah. Other people want to blow up my car," he said and laughed.

I joined him in laughter. "Well, you must be happy to run into your friend after not seeing him for a few years. I couldn't imagine not—" The words caught in my throat and choked me. I was about to say I couldn't imagine not seeing Marissa for that long before I got an invisible punch in the gut that caused me to stop talking.

"Me and that guy go way back," Jake said, unaware of my slip of the tongue. "Frank and I, we came through some muddy situations. You don't have to be in constant contact for the friendship to be real," Jake said.

I thought about it. I talked to Marissa every day, and our relationship turned out to be a horrible stain on my life. Our constant contact didn't really amount to anything in the end.

Breakfast arrived, and we ate in silence until Jake asked, "Were you serious when you agreed to go on a double date with Frank and his wife?"

"I didn't really think about it. I was just being polite," I said.

"So, you're a people pleaser?" he asked.

I tilted my head to the side and thought about it. It was close to the truth.

"Tess? Are you a people pleaser?" he pressed.

"I guess. I've always been the one to try to satisfy everyone. Maybe that's how it's easy for me to overlook things others would question. Because of my strong desire to keep the peace, I didn't confront Marissa when she wore suggestive clothes around my husband. I thought it was innocent when she said things to Amiri that were borderline flirtatious. She pushed the envelope for a friend. There were even a few times he flirted back. I just trusted that it was all innocent. I thought they would treat me as I would treat them."

"That's not how people work. You have to demand boundaries. Even then, you have to be aware they may cross the line."

"But, it's not supposed to be that way in a marriage. He wasn't supposed to cross the damn line, no matter what!" I blurted out.

"You're right," Jake said. He looked like he wanted to say more, but he dropped the subject.

My ringing phone dragged my attention to my newly set up device. I reached for it on the table. It displayed a number I didn't recognize. I wondered who would be calling the phone I had just programed.

"Hello?"

"Hello, please do not hang up on me," Marissa's aggravating voice grated out.

She must've called from someone else's phone because I wouldn't have answered I saw her number.

"What do you want, Marissa?"

"I want to apologize, for everything. What I did was wrong. It was all wrong. You were the best friend I've ever had, and I was a horrible friend to you," she said, her voice choking up on the last sentence. She sounded pitiful.

"I'm glad we cleared that up *after* I'm headed to jail. You can have him freely now, Marissa. Soon, the only phone calls I'll be able to make will be if a prison warden says it's okay for me to make them."

"Oh, Tess. I'm so sorry. Everything is just so messed up."

"I don't care if you're sorry, Marissa! My heart has never been a game for you to play. But you played me, and it's over, so there is no need for you to reach out to me, ever again. If you are trying to clear your conscience, I suggest you find a church to join. It won't be done through a heart to heart with me. I will never talk to you again, and that's a promise!"

"Do you think I meant for this to happ—"

I hung up and jumped out of my seat. I stormed toward the exit. I trekked a beeline toward my room. I had to get to a private place where I could unload my frustration and not look like a crying fool in public.

"Tess, wait," Jake said. He was close behind me. He caught up with me at the elevators and placed an arm around my shoulder.

"I just want it to stop," I said with a cracking voice. "If she were a friend, she would have never looked at my husband that way. And, if Amiri cared about me, even a little, he wouldn't have compromised the woman I called my sister."

Jake stilled me by wrapping his arms around my waist. Warmth from his body covered me. The smell of his woodsy cologne assaulted my senses taking me to another place.

"He didn't deserve you. After what you've been through in the past few years with the loss of your parents, I would have never mistreated you that way," he said, holding me closer.

I wanted to pull back, to run away, to reject him, but my need to vent was long overdue. Since the day I jumped in my car and rushed away from Atlanta, I'd been alone with no one to talk to, which left me with nothing but my thoughts of how alone I was in this world.

My hands gripped onto the fabric of the back of Jake's shirt, and I finally did it. I cried with my heart and soul. This wasn't a panicked cry about being locked up. This wasn't a cry about losing my man. This wasn't a cry about losing a friend. This wasn't even a cry about my parents being gone. This was a cry from my very being. It was all of my pains at once unlocking and freeing themselves onto Jake's shoulder. My emotions revved to a category five hurricane. I felt completely helpless to the feelings stirring inside of me.

"I don't want to go back to Atlanta. I don't want to see either of them. Please don't make me go back to that blasted city," I cried.

Jake rubbed my back until I calmed down some.

"I'm not taking you back until you're ready. In the meantime, how about we not discuss your husband or friend anymore?"

I pulled out of his arms and wiped my eyes and nose with my hands.

"Deal."

"Good. Now, hand over your phone, and let me take you for a ride."

I handed him the phone and took his outstretched hand. I didn't hesitate for a moment as he led me out of the hotel lounge into the balmy Alabama air.

We waited on the valet to bring his car around. Jake put his hand on the small of my back to help me inside the car. I didn't ask where we were headed. He could have been taking me back to Atlanta to a jail cell for all I knew. At that moment, I trusted him enough to follow wherever he led.

CHAPTER TEN

Jake

I acted irrationally. I hadn't been this foolish until I laid eyes on Tess. I never wanted to take another man's wife, and there I was in the middle of Tess's matrimonial drama and not giving one damn about being there. All I could imagine was the day I stamped my name over every inch of her body. The thought of him having a hold on her made these feelings grow stronger. Because of the strong draw I had to Tess, I should've run as far away from this woman as I could, and as fast as I could, but I didn't. I always chased the next thrill, and I was ready for the next moment I could spend with her.

"What is this place?" Tess asked, looking around the empty state park as we rode through the gates.

There were a few people riding bikes near a trail by the river and a few walking along the riverside holding hands. Other than that, the park was wildlife for as far as the eye could see. I drove until we were at the tip of Jackson's Spring Trail, parked the car, and hopped out to open Tess's door.

"We're at the park, so we can go for a walk," I told her.

"A walk? Really?" She looked around at the campgrounds and the river. "Jake, you'd better be glad I wore comfortable sandals to walk in."

Tess sounded half skeptical about the hike ahead, but there was no need for her to worry. I wouldn't let anything happen to her. I would protect her.

"I *am* glad that you wore something comfortable. I checked out your shoes before we left the hotel," I said as I held my hand out to her. "What I'm most glad about is that you agreed to come out here with me."

"Sure you are," she said, looking around once again. "You probably do these kinds of walks all the time."

"What do you mean by that?"

"The kind of walks where you take unsuspecting women on a romantic feeling stroll, get them to lower their guard down, and boom they're in your bed. And, when they wake up the next morning, you send them on their way." She had a weird look in her eyes as she basically accused me of being a dog.

"You think you know me, huh?" I asked.

"I don't know you, but I know your type."

"Wow, really? So, you're admitting that we'll end up in bed?" I asked. My wandering eyes landed on her luscious lips as I awaited her reply.

Damn, what I wouldn't do to taste her lips.

"Of course, that's not what I'm saying. If that's all you got from what I said, it must be true that you're a playboy."

Tess broke her hand free from mine and walked ahead of me. I caught up with her.

"That's not *all* I took from it. Getting you in bed is not what I'm trying to do either," I said, taking Tess's hand in mine again. "I just wanted you to come here so that you could relax. I GPS'd the nearest walking trail so we could both defuse. A nice stroll while looking out on the river usually does this for me."

She looked out at the river. Her worried facial features softened.

"Things like this help me when I'm going through something. I wanted to do the same for you," I continued. I wanted to make her feel better, though I would not stop for one moment if she agreed to get in my bed tonight.

"I have a hard time trusting people," she said, turning to me.

"I understand what you're feeling, Tess. With the way people are these days, you almost have to be that way to guard yourself," I said.

"So, do you have issues with trust?" she asked.

"Well, I have a few people I rely on—my boy, Lou, my old friend, Frank, and my mentor from the police department. Other than those three, I'm slow to trust or depend on others. I hope that will change when the right person comes along," I said and looked into her piercing brown eyes.

Her innocence was something to behold. Yet, her pouty lips begged me to devour them. I imagined the sweet taste would linger on my lips for days. Instead of feeding my desire, I walked beside her, soaking in the serene setting of nature. It felt good to share it with her.

"Well, since we're strolling on the river, we might as well get to know each other. Tell me more about you," said Tess.

"As I mentioned last night, I grew up in foster care and moved around a lot because I was a badass. No one wanted to deal with my mischievousness or my temper."

"You don't strike me as someone with a bad temper," she said.

"When people try to run over me or anyone I care about, it comes out then. As long as no one is bothering me or mine, I'm good."

"I see."

"I never met my mother or my father, so I protect the people I do have with my life," I explained.

"Do you know where your parents are now?" she asked.

"Not really, though I've been told my father is a rich billionaire that lives in Atlanta."

"A billionaire? Are you serious? Has it ever crossed your mind to look him up?" she asked.

"Not even once. I'm not in the business of looking for disappointment. He was a disappointment when he left me behind, so why would I go searching for a letdown?"

"Good point. I don't know. I couldn't imagine living in the same town as my father and not going to see him," she said.

"I'm sure there are a lot of things you could never imagine about being me," I countered.

Tess walked beside me quietly.

"What are you thinking about?" I asked.

"I don't understand how a person could walk away from their children and live in the same town and not say a word to them. That baffles my mind."

"As for my father, it's a liberating thing for me not to care if the man I bump into as I walk inside of a restaurant is my father or just some old fart who isn't paying attention. That way, I won't be able to identify the crappy person who left me in foster homes with people who treated me like shit. I know he's wealthy, and I know he's famous, but I've never asked who he is. I don't want to know," I admitted.

"I guess that's one way to handle it," she said and went quiet again.

"Yeah, sometimes it's best to let sleeping dogs lie, Tess."

"Maybe you're right," she agreed.

I smiled. "I'm always right. You'll learn that about me."

"I see," she said, smiling as well.

"Yeah, you're going to see," I told her.

We walked another quarter mile around the river in silence.

"What about your mother?" she asked, once we stopped at the pier and leaned against the rail.

"No one knows where she disappeared to. My last foster parent told me she didn't know where my mother was. She only told me my father had lots of money and that I should reach out to him. My guess was she wanted me to contact him, so he could give her money for keeping me. Thankfully, she didn't tell me his full name and what she did tell me I have erased from my memory. I don't want to know."

"That foster mom had to be a horrible person to play with your feelings like that, knowing you'd probably be rejected by your father. People can be so selfish," said Tess.

"The world is filled with selfish people. Most people have tunnel vision. If it doesn't serve them, they're not concerned."

"Don't I know it, Jake."

While Tess was looking out at the river, I stepped away from the railing and moved to stand in front of her so that I could see into her eyes. I stood close enough to her that I could feel her body heat. The burning desire to back her into the railing and assault every inch of her rose inside of me.

"Being around so many bad people taught me how to spot a good one when I saw one. When I first laid eyes on you, I already knew you were a treasure to behold," I told her.

"Jake, I'm not anyone's trea—"

I swept her into my arms and planted a lingering kiss on her lips. I slowly backed her against the rails. She didn't reject me. She opened her mouth and allowed her tongue to dance with mine in the sweetest ritual known to man. I couldn't explain what went on between us as I moved my tongue eagerly inside of her sweet mouth. I inhaled until her essence filled me. A slow moan escaped Tess's throat. I almost burst inside my pants from the sound alone. After this kiss, I never wanted to spend a moment alive that our tongues weren't connected in this sweet union. My lips traveled down to the side of her neck, tickling her soft skin with butterfly kisses.

"We should go now," she mumbled.

"No. I want to kiss you some more." I returned my kisses to her lips to suppress her words. I didn't want to stop. I didn't want to move one inch. I continued to taste her, suckling her skin into my mouth as if to register the flavor into my mind. It would never be forgotten.

"Jake, people are watching us," she mumbled against my lips. "We shouldn't do this in public. Let's go back to the hotel."

My head spun over her suggestion that we should go back to the hotel. I looked around. I saw an older couple walking by smiling at us. Yet, all I could feel was Tess. I could feel her all over me, and I wanted more.

"Your room or mine?" I asked.

"No," she chuckled. "Take me back to the hotel, and I'll go to my room, and you go to yours," Tess said, her words rivaling the heated look in her eyes.

Disappointment raked through me.

"You can't tell me you didn't just feel that between us," I said.

"Oh, I felt every bit of it, Jake, which is why we need to separate and fast."

"Tess, baby..." I protested, leaning in to breathe in the fragrance of her neck, once again.

She smiled as she took my hand. "Come on, caveman. Let's go."

"Careful with the nickname. I may just go caveman for real," I teased.

Tess started walking toward the car. I huffed out a gush of air and walked beside her. I opened her door for her, then got into the driver's seat.

On the drive to the hotel, sexual energy filled the car. I'd look at her and imagine her pinned against the car window. She would look at me and coyly turn toward the passenger window. At the hotel, I walked her to her room. Just like she said, this was where we would separate. She told me goodbye, pushed the door closed, and was about to shut me out.

"Wait," I said before her door shut all the way. "Can we get together later tonight and go out to dinner or something?"

She opened the door wider and said, "Sure. I would like that."

"I'll be back here to get you at seven, then," I replied happily.

"I'll be ready," she said, closing the door, dousing my desire to slide inside of her that very moment.

***

As I looked out over the city, I thought long and hard about what I was getting myself into. I was falling for a married woman. Her marriage was toast, but still, she had paperwork in the state of Georgia that showed another man could claim her as his. That rattled me to the core. As long as another man could step up and speak for her, I was unnerved. I turned away from the view of the ocean and waited for Tess to return from the restroom. I picked her up at seven on the dot, and we were at a nice Italian restaurant about to have dinner. I was about to pick up the menu when my eyes collided with a pair of brown slanted eyes that sent shivers running through my spine.

Tess wore a white dress that clung to her long sun-kissed thighs for dear life. She exuded sexiness. I could feel it from where I sat. What man would be stupid enough to cheat on her?

His garbage. My goddess, I thought.

"Hey, did you miss me?" she asked, teasing me with the most seductive look.

I stood and greeted her properly by pulling her into my arms and hugging her like I hadn't seen her in years. She had only left me a few minutes ago. As I released her, I noticed a tiny red mark on her right neck that made her look even more alluring. I left my mark on her when I sucked her neck at the park. I loved seeing my mark on her.

"Yes," I said, answering her question. "Every time I see you, you look amazing. How do you do it?"

"I don't know," she said humbly.

Tess smiled, blushing as I helped her into her seat. I moved from the chair across from her and sat down beside her.

"Frank texted me while you were in the bathroom and said he wanted to meet up tonight. So, I invited him and his wife to join us. I hope that's not a problem."

"No, that's not a problem."

"We'll have a little time to be alone before they get here."

"That's fine, Jake," she said, saying my name in a way that made me melt a little. I found it intriguing the way she innocently drove me mad. The smallest thing she did made me feel like I was on top of the world.

Tess looked around the dimly lit room, then shifted her attention to the menu. When she looked up from the menu, her hand reached out and touched mine. I sat silently taking in her striking beauty.

"This place is nice. I love Italian. Do you know what you want?" she asked.

Her touch caused my skin to burn instantly. I gazed into her slanted brown eyes, allowing mine to sweep over her curvaceous body. As her lips perked into a semi-smile, I couldn't help but think of the delicious way they tasted.

I bet she tastes good all over, especially in the middle, I thought.

I pulled my bottom lip into my mouth. I knew what I wanted to eat, and it wasn't on the menu.

"Good evening," the waiter approached our table, breaking my salacious stare away from Tess. "Would you like to place your drink orders now?"

"Yes, we have two more people who will join us, so, for now, I'll have whiskey on the rocks for me and—"

"I'll have a glass of your special red wine," Tess completed my sentence.

"Got it," the waiter said writing on his pad. "I will be back with your drinks shortly. The waiter walked away and disappeared behind the drink station.

"Sorry, we're late." Frank approached the table with a gorgeous young lady on his arm.

Not bad, Frank, I thought as her tight body slid into the seat Frank held out for her. The girl couldn't have been a day older than twenty one. Her flowing blond hair swooped over her perfectly tanned face that held a set of sparkling blue eyes. Her eyes sparkled as she looked at me. She caught my attention because those same blue eyes roamed all over me. I stood up and shook my friend's hand.

"No problem, bro. Glad you made it. Tess and I just ordered drinks and were thinking about getting out there on the dance floor." I pointed to the little section in the middle of the room where a few couples were dancing to slow classical music.

Tess's mouth flew open. She looked at me with confused eyes. I hadn't mentioned anything to her about dancing.

"Rachel and I may get out there in a little while. By the way, let me formally introduce my beautiful wife. Jake, meet Rachel. Rachel, meet Jake. This is my buddy's date, Tess. Tess meet Rachel."

I reached my hand out to shake Rachel's.

"Hi Rachel, you look like a pretty nice girl. How'd you end up with this guy?" I teased.

Rachel stood up, sideswiped Tess, and thrust herself into me for a hug that was way too close and lasted far too long.

"So, nice to finally meet the guy I've heard so many stories about," she purred with her arms wrapped around my neck.

I backed off.

"Nice to meet you, too, Rachel."

"She's a little clingy. Let Jake up for air," Frank joked. He stood and gently nudged his wife back into her seat.

She sat down, seductively wiggling onto the wooden chair.

"Honey, you'd better dance with that man if he wants to dance," Rachel said as her greeting to Tess. "Take it from me. One day, they just stop wanting to do everything with you, especially after you have their children."

Frank looked uncomfortable as his wife mocked him. It was an awkward introduction to her, to say the least. I waited for my boy to respond. It wasn't like him to roll over for anyone, but he never said a word. The only thing I could surmise was he was in the dog house for something he'd done wrong. If that's what marriage did to a man, I sure didn't want it.

I could tell what Rachel said rubbed Tess the wrong way. She faked a smile and didn't respond. I wrapped my arm around Tess's seat protectively.

"I don't think that'll be a problem for us. We're good, whether Tess wants to dance or not," I interjected.

"Well, I'm just saying. What one woman won't do…" Rachel let the meaning of her words linger in the air.

I could feel my blood boiling. She unknowingly said things that could trigger bad memories for my woman. *My woman.* Did I just claim her? Yes, I did, and I took no reservations in doing so.

"I think I'd like take that dance," Tess said.

"Yeah, I think we should dance." I stood to my feet to help pull out her chair. I took her hand and guided her to the floor, leaving Frank and his wife with scowls on their faces. Frank scowled at his wife for her inappropriate outburst, and Rachel, I didn't know what the hell her problem was.

Once we arrived onto the dance floor, Tess said in awe, "She's unbelievably attracted to you. She can't even hide it in front of her husband."

"Man, that was so weird. I don't think she wants me like that though."

"Yeah, well, take it from me. The woman is a man-eater, and you're on the menu. Look, she's checking you out now."

I watched Tess smirk. I planned to kiss it away from her lips before the night was over. I slowly turned and looked toward our table. Frank was checking out the menu. However, his wife had a menu in her hand, peaking over it and looking directly at me. *What the fuck? I don't need this kind of drama in my life, now or never,* I fumed internally.

"I told you," Tess said, giggling as she held onto my neck.

I tilted my head, looking away from Rachel's mischievous glare. I kept moving Tess and I side to side to keep up with the beat.

"My boy has his hands filled with her," I said.

"And that's saying the least about it," Tess agreed.

"The thing is," I whispered close to Tess's ear. "I'm not concerned about his dilemma. I'm more concerned about how you will treat me after you have my children."

"Jake! Stop saying things like that. We've only known each other a few days. Besides, I thought you were only here as a good Samaritan to help me get out of trouble."

I stepped back to look into her eyes.

"That's true. It's also true that from the first night I saw you I wanted you. It was fate that I ended up in that car garage at the very moment you came out. You see, this has nothing to do with your case and everything to do with us being where we're supposed to be."

I wrapped my arms around Tess's waist and slowly turned her so that she was standing with her backside facing my front. Her soft ass melded into me, and all my blood rushed south. I could feel the soft trembles in her spine. I knew she would respond to me like that. The past was just that…the past. I planned to show her a better future. I rocked Tess in my arms until we faced away from our table.

"What's happening between us, baby, is going to be so much more than your case in Atlanta," I assured her.

Tess turned in my arms, staring into my eyes. We stood there reading each other for a full minute before I couldn't take it any longer. The hesitation I sensed in her made me dip my head down to capture her lips, only to be met by her placing two fingers against mine. She closed her eyes, looking as if it took everything in her to reject our undeniable connection.

"Not here," she said, then took my hand and started walking back toward the table.

I followed behind her, watching her ass sway from side to side like a sick little puppy. I wanted her so badly that I could feel it in my bones. As soon as I sat down, I flagged the waiter over so we could order our entrée. After we ordered, Frank sparked up a conversation.

"Jake, man, how long has it been since we were out there trying our best to be men in blue?"

"It's been six, maybe seven years. I don't know. It was a long time. Long enough for you to become an old man," I told Frank, which caused Tess to giggle. It was a harmless joust that had Frank laughing, as well.

"You said that right. He *is* an old man. His aging is starting to show, too," Rachel said in a harsh tone. All lightness of our conversation left the table.

"I wouldn't say all that," Tess chimed in. "He looks really good to me. You have a handsome and fine man that any woman would be lucky to have. Maybe you shouldn't be so quick to say things like that about him in another woman's presence. Like you said, what one woman won't do…" Tess looked at Rachel as if challenging her to a side street brawl.

Fire rose from the pits of my soul over the way she complimented my friend in front of me. My rational side knew she was only trying to prove a point to his rude wife, but my primal side didn't want to hear her say anything about how good another man looked. I felt this double date was heading downhill. Rachel's sour attitude only made matters worse. This wasn't what I planned when I asked Tess out.

"Tess and I have a big day ahead of us tomorrow. I'll have to meet up with you before I leave town, Frank," I said, standing to my feet. I then helped Tess from her seat.

"You're leaving?" Frank asked.

"Yeah, we're going to head out."

"But, your food hasn't come yet," Frank said, sounded deflated.

"Man, you have some things to work out with the wife. Just tell the waiter to send our food back, and here's the money for it." I dropped a few bills on the table.

"Alright. I understand," Frank said, looking at his wife with displeasure. "I'll call you soon, man." Frank extended his hand to shake mine. He then pulled me into a brotherly hug.

"Talk to you then, man," I said, securing Tess's hand in mine and briskly walking out into the warm night's air. I breathed in the balmy air and thought about the way Frank's wife disrespected him and the compliments Tess gave him.

"Thanks for getting me out of there. I don't like women like her," Tess said, taking the thoughts right out of my mind.

"I don't either, but he married her. There's something about her that he likes or liked," I reasoned.

"Yeah, she's young, blond, and fit. He liked banging her. Now, he's getting to see who she really is," said Tess.

"Well, he'll have to deal with her attitude. If I know my friend, it will be soon. But, what's most important is that you don't call another man sexy in front of me again."

"What are you talking about? I didn't call him sexy." Tess laughed.

"Well, you said he was handsome, fine, and looked good to you."

She had this cunning look in her eyes as she smiled at me.

"Are you jealous?"

"Not for long. I'm going to make you pay for that."

"Oh, so it's like that?"

"Get your pretty self in the car," I said before helping her inside.

I drove back to the hotel and convinced Tess to ditch her shoes and take a walk on the beach with me. We held hands and looked out at the peaceful waters.

"It's just so beautiful," she said of the sight before us. The moon peeked out from the other side of the ocean, making it look like a beautiful portrait drawn just for us.

I scanned the beach area. It was empty except for a few couples sharing intimate time. They were far away from where we were. I grabbed ahold of her face and kissed her lips. I wrapped an arm around her waist and pulled her close to me. I sat down in the sand and pulled Tess on top of me. I flipped over on top of her and peppered soft kisses all over her until I reached the fabric at the juncture between her thighs.

"I want you so bad!" I groaned.

"Jake... we...Jake... Jake, I—" she whispered, holding on to the sides of her dress.

I inhaled her womanly scent deep into my lungs.

"God, you smell so good," I said.

A pleasurable sigh escaped her lips when I slowly lifted her dress and grazed my lips against her thighs. Her hands left the fabric of her dress and ran through my close-cropped hair, lifting my head so that our eyes met. The hunger in her eyes challenged my restraint. I wanted to plummet into her at that very moment. She wriggled beneath me, and any control I had drifted away with the next wave of the ocean.

"Jake, we shouldn't do this outside," she whispered, yet the sensual movement of her body said otherwise.

My eyes greedily ate up the sight of what was underneath her dress. I dipped my head between her thighs and swiped my tongue across her panties. I stuck my thumbs on either side of her panties and slid them down past her knees.

She opened her mouth to speak. I covered her body with mine and shoved my tongue back into her mouth, kissing her speechless. I trailed kisses back down to her slit and began stroking her clit.

"We should—Oh, my. That feels so good," Tess murmured. Her legs trembled.

I wanted to take her back to my bed. But, God knows I had zero ability to control my actions. I held my desire at bay for as long as possible. I pushed her panties further down her legs. I yanked them off, took a long whiff from the moist center of her black lace thong, and smiled in splendid pleasure. Once my nostrils were filled with her scent, I stuffed her panties into my pocket.

They were mine to keep. She was mine, too. She just didn't know it yet.

"Jake, we can't—" she said, trying to regain control of this situation that was definitely not controllable.

"Watch me." I dipped down once again to kiss her beautiful lower lips before easing up her body to kiss her mouth.

I made love to her mouth, mixing the taste of whiskey, wine, and her sticky juices, making the best blend of a love drug ever created. Her constant moans into my mouth affirmed she wanted this as much as I did.

"Let's go inside," she moaned.

As much as I wanted to take her right there, I stood and reached a hand out for her. "Come."

Tess took my hand, stood up, and adjusted her dress.

We knocked the sand off our clothes before walking toward the hotel.

CHAPTER ELEVEN

Tess

"Take me home," I told Jake.

My mind was blown by our beachside make out session. It was best to put space between us. When Jake was near me, on top of me, and all over me, there was no way I could deny him. How could I when I couldn't even think straight?

Had he not stopped when he did, my legs would be spread eagle for anyone on the beach to see. That's how unbelievably irresistible the moment had been and how much I needed that type of affection. I couldn't think like a rational adult around him.

"So, you're leaving me?" he asked, sounding deflated.

"Yes, I need to think about everything. It's all happening so fast. I want to make sure I don't jump into something without knowing what it is."

"I can tell you right now that it's special. I've had many flings I'm not proud of, but I've never been instantly connected to a woman like I am with you," he said, as he stroked the side of my face with his hand.

"Jake, you know my situation. I haven't even signed my divorce papers."

"But, you have them, Tess."

"Yes, and I need to go home and sign them and put them in the mail. I just think we should do things in order."

Jake relented. "Okay, Tess. Since you insist on going back to your place, I'll take you there and stay with you tonight."

"You're not listening to what I'm saying. I think I should stay there alone, Jake."

"If it's because you think things will go too far, I respect your wishes. I'll sleep on the sofa."

I sighed. He wasn't getting it. We walked back to the car, hopped in and started toward my house, which was only about ten minutes away. Once we arrived, Jake got out and helped me out of my seat then planted another mind-numbing kiss on my lips.

"See, this is exactly the reason I have to get away from you," I said, breaking away from the kiss.

"I promise not to bother you if I stay the night. I'll sleep on the couch, and you won't even know I'm here," he said.

"With that look on your face, I know you don't believe a word you're saying. You look like you're about to eat me up right now."

"I don't bite, baby."

"Somehow, I find that extremely unbelievable."

"I don't want to leave you, Tess."

"I'll be fine, Jake."

"But, what about me? I won't be fine," he said.

"You'll be fine, too, Jake." Tess giggled.

"At least let me check out your place and make sure no one is in there. That's the only way I'll be able to rest tonight."

I shook my head but gave in.

"Come on in, Jake."

After Jake checked my house for safety, he kissed me silly on the doorstep. It was a struggle to watch him leave, but I let him go and fell back on my sofa. I texted Jake a goodnight message. He let me know he'd made it back to his hotel and would love to come back over. I smiled but declined.

I was getting comfortable on the sofa when I heard a noise near the front door. I thought Jake had come back anyway.

Dang, he's persistent.

"Jake?"

The door handle turned, and the door slowly slid open.

I jolted.

"Amiri! What in the hell are you doing? You have no business breaking into my parents' house," I yelled at a dumbfounded looking Amiri.

"I came to talk to you, Tess," he slurred.

"No. What you need to do is leave, quick, fast and in a hurry!" I walked toward my bedroom to be closer to my gun. I felt jumpy after the way he broke in. I kicked off my shoes, for no other reason than feeling nervous.

"Tess, you're so beautiful. I miss you so much, baby," he said, walking toward me. Amiri had a look that told me he wanted to be intimate. He also looked and sounded like he'd had far too many drinks. It was a wonder he even made it to Gulf Shores without killing himself.

I have to admit that part of me thought I would be elated when I saw him again. Yet, I loathed the sight of his face. He had unkempt hair riding along the sides of his face as his cheeks went up into a smile. The striking handsomeness that used to hit me as soon as I saw him was gone. He was still muscular with a rock-hard body that made ladies turn their heads, but it didn't attract me like it used to. Everything about Amiri repulsed me now. The sight of him standing in front of me with his alcohol breath striking me in the face was enough to make my stomach churn.

"I didn't break in, Tess. I used our spare key."

"I didn't give you a key, so you shouldn't have a *spare* key."

"You left it in our old house. I found it yesterday as I was unpacking some things into my apartment. I probably shouldn't have used it to come in, but I needed to talk to you. You wouldn't have let me in if I didn't have it," he acknowledged.

"That's right. I would not have let you in my house. Since you already know this, you can leave now," I yelled.

"I can't do that. Not until we talk."

"I don't want to talk to you, Amiri."

"Tess, I gave you the time you needed. I even foolishly thought I could let you go, but today I realize I can't live without you," Amiri said, taking steps toward me. "I don't want a divorce. We have to work this out, baby."

"What made you come to the realization that you can't live without me? Is your side chick too pregnant for you?" I pushed him away and walked toward the door headed to the living room.

My phone rang, stopping me in my tracks. I reached over and grabbed it off my dresser. Amiri caught my hand and turned the phone over.

"I didn't know you had a new phone," he said, surprised.

"I didn't know I had to tell you anything that I do." I snatched my hand away from his, looked at the caller ID, and swiped the phone to answer it. By that time, it was on its sixth ring. "Hello," I answered, sounding frustrated.

Amiri, who was one inch away from my face, started screaming at me.

"Hang up that damn phone and talk to me, Tess," he slurred. He grabbed the phone out of my hands and held it high in the air to where I couldn't reach it. "Baby, whoever this is can wait. We need to talk."

"Get out of here, Amiri!" I yelled.

"I can't let you go. I just can't do that," he said.

I took a few deep breaths and tried another approach with him.

"Give me back my phone, Amiri," I said calmly.

"No!" Amiri swiped the screen sideways to end the call.

He never put his hands on me while we were married. Yet, the way he scowled made me think he would hit me.

"Get out now, or I'm calling the police."

"You're not calling anyone," he said, closing the space between us. He slithered his arms around my waistline and pulled me to him. "I need you, Tess. I can't live without you. Please, let me make it right. Let's spend the night together and see if you still want me to go tomorrow."

"Amiri, the ways you have hurt me could never be fixed by spending a night together. Never."

"Tess." My name lingered in the air from the way he said it. It sounded the same way he used to sound when he was in a vulnerable position as we made love. As much as Amiri repulsed me because of what he did to me, that sound reminded me that at one time I loved him to no end. I wrestled to get out of his grasp and away from him forever.

"Don't call my name like that. You have no right to say my name like that. You gave that right away when you decided to sleep with her." I couldn't even say her name without my flesh crawling. The sound of each syllable hurt me deeply.

Amiri removed his grip from my waist, allowing me to break free from him. "Baby, I'm sorry for everything I have done. I was a very selfish man, but I never meant to hurt you. I know my faults, and I have changed."

"What's done is done, Amiri. I don't want to hear any excuses or any reasoning. The only reason I'm here right now and not at a hotel across town is because I came here to sign the divorce papers you sent me. Those papers make everything final. We are done."

"What are you saying? You haven't been staying here, Tess? Who are you staying at a hotel with?" Amiri asked. He sounded wounded.

"Again, none of your business."

"Where have you been staying, Tess?"

"Amiri, don't ask me questions."

I stormed away from him as fast as I could. I went into the dining room to get the package he sent me. It was on the kitchen table. I removed the divorce papers and picked up the pen I had beside them.

"I should have done this when you sent them to me," I told him. I placed the pen onto the paper to sign my name. I had never been so sure that we were done until he showed up.

Amiri gently laid his hand on top of mine.

"Don't."

Hearing that one compound word, my heart broke in two. He didn't say much yet said a lot. Singing divorce papers was something I never thought I would do in a million years. Divorce wasn't an option when he took my hand in his vowed to love and cherish me above all others. A part of me hadn't been able to process the finality of signing those papers. I couldn't bring myself to end our marriage. I didn't have the fortitude to push the pen across the paper. Now that he held my hand in his, begging me not to sign, I felt weak all over again.

There were moments I thought to have him back was all I wanted...all I needed. Yet, I felt empty standing next to the same man who once filled my life with happiness. With tears in my eyes, I faced Amiri.

"I never wanted this...any of it. All I wanted was to love you like you were the last man alive. All I wanted was to cherish you like you were the best man alive. Because, to me, you were. I put my trust, faith, and future in your hands, and you balled your fist up and crumpled all three."

"I know, baby. I know," he said, breaking down to his knees to cry. "I have done so much to hurt you. Please—"

"No, Amiri. We can't get past this. Not this, not ever."

Reaching a point of finality isn't always something a woman is aware of, but at that moment I knew I'd reached that point. The truth is, had Amiri had an affair with any other woman, time and commitment would have made me consider a second chance for our marriage. The betrayal of him being with Marissa was a deal breaker for life. More tears sprang out of my eyes, which was an indication that I was bawling. Amiri stood to his feet and swiped his eyes with his hands. He, too, had real tears.

"I guess I'll just have to deal with the mess I've made of things," he said and started pacing toward the door. He stumbled when his leg sideswiped one of the chairs in the kitchen and nearly fell. I reached to help steady him, and he damn near brought me down with him.

"I'm sorry, Tess. I think I had one too many."

"You think?" I laughed.

"Yeah." He laughed.

"You know what? Just lie down on the sofa and get some rest tonight. You can leave in the morning," I said.

"Are you sure I can't sleep with you?" he pressed.

"Don't push it, Amiri Knox. I'm only offering you shelter so you can sleep off your liquor before you get on the road. I may be pissed to high hell with you, but I don't want you to kill yourself on the highway. I can be a bitch but not that bitch. Though, if you push me, I'll put you on the front porch to sleep out there."

He raised his hands in the air. "Alright, alright. I'll sleep on the couch. I did drink too much, and that's not even like me."

What is like you these days? I wanted to ask, but I left it at that.

Amiri laid down on the sofa. I went to the hallway closet to get him a blanket and pillow. By the time I got back into the living room, he was already asleep, and someone was banging on the front door like they were the police.

CHAPTER TWELVE

Jake

I took off my pants and shirt. I went into the bathroom to shower. After taking a warm shower, I walked back out into my hotel room to get ready for bed. I checked my cell. There was a text from Tess telling me good night. I texted her back, once again asking if she was sure she didn't want me to come back over. She shot me down again, so I turned on my laptop and logged onto my email. There was a message from Jarrod at the police department telling me to bring Tess in to speak with the district attorney. He said the DA's office would drop the case against her as long as she paid for the repairs on Lexington's destroyed property. Apparently, they had to reconstruct the wall in Amiri's office, as well as replace some office furniture she shot up. Excited to tell her the good news, I picked up my cell and dialed her number. It took a while, but she finally answered.

"Hello," her lovely voice chimed in my ear, instantly making me smile.

"Hang up that damn phone and talk to me, Tess!" a man yelled, his words slurring. "Baby, whoever this is can wait. We need to talk."

"Get out of here, Amiri!" Tess yelled.

"Tess, Tess? Are you there? Is that Amiri at your house?" I yelled into the phone.

"I can't let you go. I just can't do that," the man said. It was obvious neither of them had the phone to their ears.

"Give me back my phone, Amiri," Tess said. The franticness in her voice wiped away the good mood I had when I dialed her number.

"No!" the man yelled, and the line went dead.

I dialed her number over and over as I dressed. It went straight to voicemail. I was in my car driving toward Tess's place in a matter of a minute. I drove so fast that if a cop clocked me I would go to jail for reckless endangerment. All I could think was, if Amiri put one hand on my woman, I was going to break him in two.

I broke every traffic law on the way. Within five minutes, I pulled into Tess's driveway and parked. I dashed toward the porch to check things out. The lights were on inside. Nothing looked out of the ordinary. I turned the doorknob, which was locked. There was no evidence of a break-in, so hopefully, that meant Tess was safe inside. I knocked on the door eager to get inside. After there was no answer, I banged on the door loudly. I put my ear to the door to see if I could hear any sounds coming from the house.

"Tess! Tess!" I yelled.

As I was considering kicking the door in, it flung open, and Tess was standing there with a blanket in her hand.

"Jake. I was just about to call you back."

"Are you okay?" I said, passing by her and looking around the foyer and into the house. "When we were on the phone, I heard a man yelling in the background. I came as fast as I could."

By the time I finished my sentence, I spotted the culprit. Amiri was lying on the sofa with his eyes closed.

"What is he doing here?" I asked Tess.

Tess closed the front door. She walked over to stand beside me as I looked at Amiri.

"He came a little while after you left. He said he wanted to talk. I told him to leave, and he was about to leave, but he fell over the table. He's drunk, so I told him to sleep it off on the couch," she said.

"Why was he yelling at you? Did he put his hands on you?" I asked as I looked her over, observing every inch. If Amiri harmed one hair on her body, I would wake his drunk ass up and pummel him back to sleep.

"No, I'm fine," Tess said. She walked over to cover Amiri with the blanket she was holding. "He's a lot of things, but he's not crazy enough to put his hands on me," she assured.

"I'm not leaving you alone with him tonight. That's not even a discussion," I said.

"What?" Tess asked, dumbfounded. "It's not like anything's going to happen. Besides, this is my house. I get to decide who's going to stay here," she said with an attitude.

"I know whose house it is, and I know nothing is going to happen because I'll be here with you," I asserted.

"Whatever, Jake," she said dismissively and walked toward her room. "I don't have the strength for another argument. You can come back here and sleep on the recliner."

"Glad we agree," I said as I followed behind her.

There was no way I would walk back out of this house with that creep Amiri lying on the sofa.

She yawned. "Look, this has been a long day. At this point, I just want to take a shower, lay down, and go to sleep."

"Go ahead and grab your shower, and I'll tuck you in," I said, sitting down on the edge of her bed and making myself comfortable.

Tess shook her head. "No, you're sleeping on the recliner. So, get over there," she fussed.

I watched her stroll into the bathroom. I heard the shower water running. I pulled off my t-shirt and kicked out of my shoes. I tried to make myself comfortable in the recliner, but it must've been designed for a kid. That thing was so small that my legs hung over the footrest by at least a foot.

When Tess walked back into the room, thirty minutes later, I was sitting on the side of the bed waiting for her. I sucked in a deep breath when she stood in front of me wearing only a short gown. I backed up to the center of the bed.

"Come on, baby. Let's get that rest you were talking about," I said.

"Jake, what are you doing in my bed?" she asked.

"Well, as you can see I'm a tall man. That recliner is too little for me. And, I can't sleep on the couch, can I?"

She looked at the recliner then back to me.

"I guess you can't sleep on the couch," she said, looking around as if she could figure another place for me to sleep.

"Tess, it's only one bedroom in here, so I have to sleep in here," I told her.

Finally, she started walking toward the bed. She stood on the side of the bed looking down at me before sliding under the covers.

"Since we're in here together, I guess we can talk some more," she said.

I slid closer to her and wrapped an arm around her.

"We can talk," I said as one of my hands moved to her voluptuous breasts. I groaned out my satisfaction of the feel of her beautiful breasts in my hands. A part of me wanted to snap out of her spell before I climbed on top of her and took her fast and rough. I couldn't stop touching her. I wanted Tess more than I wanted anything in that moment.

"I didn't mean that kind of talking," she whined. "Jake, are you naked?"

"Yes, I like to sleep naked, baby. What do you want to talk about?" I hovered over her and asked.

My head slid down her body, tongue licking her flesh as I traveled southward. I sought out every contour of her chocolate skin and made my best attempt to taste it all.

"I   don't   know.   We   can   talk a…bout…maybe…we…um…" Tess gave up when I reached her prized possession.

My mouth opened wide and sucked her plump lips. Then, my tongue found great satisfaction in attacking her clit with masterful precision. I moved it from the hood to the hilt until an explosion erupted from her sweet lips, releasing a creamy sweetness that I lapped up like a dog.

"Oh, Jake!" she said my name, along with a host of other sexual things that drove me mad.

It took everything in me not to mount her and pound her into oblivion. I eased up her body and captured her mouth for another soul-searing kiss.

"Now that I've tasted you, I'll never get enough of you," I said.

I hunched back on my knees and scooped her into my arms. I sat her on top of me. She slid atop of me like a rider mounting her bull. She wrapped her soft legs tightly around my waist. As she slid down, I thrust inside of her, tearing away any resistance as I entered her.

"Fuck!" she growled as I began to move inside of her inch by inch. She moaned out my name and dipped her head down to kiss me.

"Tess, baby…you're so tight. You feel so good," I whispered against her soft lips. I maneuvered until she was lying on her back, and I was on top.

The sound of her moans ricocheted through my body. I began pounding into her heated flesh without restraint.

"Oh! Oui! Oh shit," she screamed out passionately.

"Am I hurting you, baby?" I asked as my rod touched the most intimate places inside of her.

She moved underneath me, only gasping out her reply.

It was all so erotic that I didn't know how much more I could take.

"Do you like that, Tess?" I asked, ramming into her slick heat to prove how perfectly we fit.

"Yes, I love it, Jake. I love it. Oh, my God, I love it."

When she locked her legs around my waist and pulled me further inside of her, I was about to erupt.

"Sweet baby," I howled, not caring if anyone heard me.

Tess pulled my face to hers and plunged her tongue inside of my mouth. She made love to my mouth before kissing my neck. She moved down to plant kisses on my chest. I gasped aloud as pleasure took over my being.

"I'm cumming, Tess. Cum with me, baby," I said as a ripple of jerking movements took over me. I sought out her lips for a kiss that held our moans and groans on one wavelength as I spasmed inside of her.

A massive gush of my seed bathed her heated walls. At the same time, her juices sprang forward, and we fused as one. Eventually, I eased out of her. I laid back on the bed, pulling her close to me. I kissed her shoulders and held onto her tight. All that mattered to me at that moment was Tess.

CHAPTER THIRTEEN

Tess

I awoke with the sun peeking through the thick draperies. A broad smile spread across my lips. Jake woke me up so many times last night to make love I should've been exhausted. Instead, I vibrantly basked in the beautiful moments we created. For the first time in a long time, I just lived in the moment. I allowed myself to be free from my past. I didn't even think about Amiri asleep on the living room sofa as Jake claimed my body. I hoped he didn't hear us, but I also didn't care if he did. Other people's feelings didn't matter. Just mine and Jake's in those heated moments. I turned over and noticed he was still asleep. His light snores made me smile. I had time to take a refreshing shower to give me life for the day ahead. After showering, I put on an oversized t-shirt, got back in bed and waited for Jake to wake up.

"Good morning," he said, reaching his arm back around my waist. "How long have you been awake, baby?"

"Just a little while. I got up and showered. I've just been waiting for you to wake up."

"Well, you should have woke me up when you got up. We could have showered together," he said.

"You were sleeping so peacefully. I didn't want to bother you."

"Really? To get in the shower with you, I would have come alive, baby."

I giggled. I was too sore to think of showering with Jake. The point of the shower was to soothe some of my aches.

"Was I snoring?" he asked. "I've been told that I snore."

"Well, about that," I said and laughed.

Jake flipped himself on top of me and pinned me down to the bed. He tickled me, which made me laugh even more.

"You're laughing at me?" he asked, tickling me ferociously.

The giggles that escaped me were uncontrollable.

"Jake! Please stop," I begged between laughs.

"Beg me!"

"I already am. Please, I'm sorry for laughing at you," I said while continuing to laugh.

He tickled me hard. It was so funny that I almost burst. I didn't even know I was ticklish.

"Ouch!" I screamed, feigning an injury to my side where his big hands were rubbing in search of a laugh.

He stopped tickling me. "Are you okay, babe?" he asked.

"Ouch, my side," I continued to fake.

It backfired when his head disappeared underneath my t-shirt and began kissing my side.

"What time are we supposed to be at breakfast this morning?" I asked, knowing we didn't have a timeframe for eating breakfast.

Jake kept his head under my shirt, kissing one side and moving across my stomach to the other side. "Whenever you want to eat, pretty woman," he murmured between kisses. "I don't need food," he added.

"Well, I'm hungry."

"Oh, and I intend to feed you." He kissed my pretend injured side once more, slowly and sensually.

Damn, I started aching for real, but only because I wanted more. His head came from underneath my shirt.

"Do we have to eat food? Because I have a taste for something else," he asked.

"Jake." I reached out and touched his face. "We need to get out of this bed before…" I said, trying to hide the desire in my voice.

"Before what? I do this?" Jake lifted one of my thighs up on his shoulder. "Or this?" He hoisted up the other.

"Jake…breakfast…" I said when his tongue swiped across my lower lips.

"I'm having mine now."

"Jaaaeeke! Come on, baby."

"Okay, your wish is my command," he said pushing up on his arms and staring down at me. "If it's food you want, it's food you'll get."

I could see the passionate look in Jake's eyes as he stared at me. He slid off of me and out of bed. He went into the bathroom and stood over the toilet, without closing the door. I could see his long, hard manhood hanging over the toilet as he relieved himself, and damn if I didn't want him back all over me, taking me like he did last night. I was just too sore already.

"What do you want me to cook?" I asked as I forced myself to walk up the hall to the kitchen.

"I'm not choosy, but if you make eggs, I only eat the whites," Jake yelled from the bathroom.

Once I got to the living room, I stopped. I looked over at the sofa where Amiri had been asleep. The covers were laying over the edge of the couch, and he was gone. I didn't want to think of it, but a part of me wondered if Amiri had heard me and Jake making love and left with his pride tucked between his legs. That would be the only reason he would leave without knocking on my bedroom door to say goodbye. The thought of him hearing me make love to another man caused my mood to flatline. We were divorcing, so what I did wasn't wrong per se. However, I didn't like the feeling of intermixing the two relationships.

I walked into the kitchen. Jake was sitting at the table.

"I guess he got up early and left," Jake said uncaringly.

"Yeah, I guess he did."

I stopped at the table, the same table I'd sat for thirty long days grieving the end of my marriage. I picked up the pen and signed the divorce papers. I slid them in the extra envelope and took them out to the mailbox. When I got back inside, I began to prepare breakfast for Jake.

"Do you have any regrets about last night?" Jake asked.

"No, not at all," I replied easily.

"Good, because I don't care if he heard us. I hope he did, and that he knows I'm going to make love to you like that over and over as long as you're mine." Jake came and stood behind me.

He wrapped his arms around my waist and kissed the sides of my neck. "I promise to hold you tight, Tess. I'm not letting you go."

"Jake, I appreciate every moment we've spent together. Thank you for being here for me during this tough time. I wish I met you at a time when I wasn't dealing with baggage, but I want to see how things go with us," I admitted to Jake.

He was a possessive brute, but he was growing on me by the moment. Any expert would tell me to take things slow with him, but it felt right to at least see where things could go.

Jake snapped his fingers. "Which reminds me of why I called you last night in the first place. I have some good news, baby," he said, smiling.

"What is it?" I asked, feeling myself get excited. I didn't even know why.

"The DA is willing to drop all charges. She wants to have someone from her office meet with you and go over the details."

"Oh, that really is good news," I beamed. "What do I have to do?"

"Basically, she wants you to agree to fix any damages to the building. They had to rebuild the wall and put in new office furniture."

"It was that bad, huh?" I said, frowning.

"Yeah, but this is nothing compared to you going to jail."

"I can pay for the repairs. No problem," I said.

"We'll get that part handled. Right now, the plan is to go back to Atlanta and square everything away with your case, and then it's all about us getting to know each other better." Jake sat down and pulled me down onto his lap.

"I like the sound of that."

CHAPTER FOURTEEN

Amiri

I sat up and stretched. I felt like I went bungee jumping and landed bluntly on my head. I forced my hurting eyes open and looked around the room. For the first few seconds, I didn't even remember where I was. *How the hell did I get here?* I wondered. Then, my memory slowly came back. I drove to Gulf Shores to get Tess back. I remembered sitting at a bar a few miles away from Tess's beach house, while I tried to get up the nerve to come here and beg her to take me back. I sat at that bar tossing back drinks until they refused to serve me any more alcohol.

When I got to Tess's house, I used the key I had and came inside. Tess wasn't happy to see me, and we argued. I was about to leave, but she realized how intoxicated I was, so she put me to sleep on her couch.

All of which led to the moment when I woke up to the sound of my wife screaming out another man's name and apparently the sounds of that man grunting and growling like he was an ax murderer. I jumped up from the sofa and ran toward her room. Ready to deal with an intruder, I revved back to thrust through the door with all my weight. That's when the man said something that blew me back.

"Am I hurting you, baby?" he asked before growling out how good Tess felt to him.

Then, Tess gasped loudly.

The man's voice grated out again, *"Do you like that, Tess?"*

Something told me to turn the doorknob. It was an overwhelming urge to see it with my own eyes. I turned the knob. To my surprise, the door opened. I peeked my head into the doorway and saw a white man long stroking my wife as if his life depended on it. My mind went wild seeing a man partake in a privilege that used to belong to me exclusively. Something broke inside of me as a man watching him make love to her. All hope was lost when I heard Tess screaming out into the night. She knew I was in that house but could care less if I listened to her passionate cries.

"Yes, I love I, Jake! I love it. Oh, my God, I love it..." she screamed over and over until I fell back against the wall from the impact of those words.

The impact of seeing my wife, well ex-wife now, making love to another man was enough force to sling me halfway down the hall. As much as I wanted to barge into that room and claim her as mine, my dirty deeds were what brought me to be a spectator to Tess's sexual tryst.

All signs of my intoxication had worn off just from what I'd seen. It was easy for me to lay down with Marissa over and over while I was married to Tess. But seeing Tess under another man was enough to bring me to my knees.

Before I broke down or reacted out of emotion, I gathered my few belongings, keys and shoes, and slithered out of that house with my heart and soul in my pocket.

CHAPTER FIFTEEN

Jake

"I have someone I need to tell you about," I said to Tess on the ride back to Atlanta.

She looked at me as if she were waiting on the other shoe to drop.

"Who is she?" she asked with an attitude.

"A young lady who caught a bad rap with her boyfriend. She called me to bond her out and, after talking to her for a while, I told her how to get out of the trouble she was in. To do that, she had to tell on her boyfriend. He threatened to retaliate against her, so I invited her to stay with me until she gets her stuff together."

"Oh," Tess said pensively. "So, you two are—"

"No, we're not seeing each other. I'm only helping her out. She shouldn't be there long, but I want you to know what's going on. I don't want any surprises to come up on my end. I'm going to be open and honest with you about everything. Tiffany will be staying in my guest bedroom until she gets back on her feet."

"Jake, that's nice of you. Have I told you that you are a great man?"

I stuck my chest out.

"You have, but you can tell me again, and I won't object."

"You are a great man. I can only imagine the people you've helped out in your lifetime."

"Well, usually, I don't invite anyone from my job into my home, but Tiffany is different. You'll see when you meet her. She's the kind of bright young woman that makes you want to step in and say there's something better out there for you. I believe she'll realize it one day."

"Uh, like what you did for me?"

"Nothing like what I did for you. I did so much more for and *to* you," I said and watched her honey brown skin tone turn red. She looked gorgeous when she blushed.

"Get your mind out of the gutter, Jake. I wasn't talking about that part. I was talking about you getting her out of trouble and helping her with a fresh start."

"I know what you meant, and I guess you're right, Tess."

"Listen Jake, I'm not trying to be funny or anything. Since you already have a houseguest, how about I stay at the Hilton? I'll get a room there for a few nights while I'm in town, and we'll hook up when we can," Tess said as we crossed the Alabama/Georgia border.

"Baby, I guess you don't know that you're mine. We're not hooking up. You're staying with me the whole time." I thought I had drilled into her that she was mine the night before. I guess I had more work to do.

"Jake, you are too much. I just don't want to intrude."

"Nonsense. I will not let you stay at a hotel while I have a perfectly good bed for you to lay in. You're coming to my condo, and I'm not taking no for an answer."

"I wasn't trying to sound like I don't want to be with you. I'm just trying to stay out of the way. And, do you have to be so pushy?"

I pulled the car off to the side of the road, put on the hazard lights, and shut off the engine. I dragged her chin so that she was facing me.

"What did you just say?"

"Do you have to be so pushy?"

"The answer to that is yes, but I was talking about the other part of what you said, Tess."

"What, that I'm trying to stay out of the way?" she repeated.

I leaned over and kissed her, hungrily drinking from her lips.

"You could never be in my way. I don't ever want to hear you say that again. You are the absolute opposite of in the way. Everywhere I am is where I want you to be." I kissed her long enough and told her enough times that I was keeping her with me. I cranked the car and continued toward Atlanta.

"Jake, I'm starting to think I'll never win an argument with you," she said, her eyes shimmering with a special glow as she smiled.

"If it's an argument about leaving my side, I'll never let you win," I assured her.

We walked through the door about an hour later to find Tiffany and Lou sitting on the sofa watching TV.

"Jake!" Tiffany said, springing to her feet as fast as her pregnant body would allow.

"Hey Tiffany, this is Tess. Tess, this is my homeboy Lou and Tiffany."

"Hey, Jake man. Glad you're back. I was just about to leave and handle some business at the office. Now, I can do it without worrying about Tiff being alone," Lou said as a greeting. "Oh, and Frank called. He says it's important that you call him."

"Okay man, thanks for keeping everything together while I was gone."

"Anytime boss man, anytime," Lou said then turned to Tiffany. "Talk to you soon."

"Okay," Tiffany said, sounding giddy.

"Tess, you want to hang out with Tiffany for a while and get to know her while I go see what's up with Frank?" I asked.

"Sure," Tess answered.

I kissed her lips and hugged her.

"Nice meeting you, Tess," Lou said on his way out.

"Same here," Tess said to Lou. Then, she went over and started talking to Tiffany on the sofa.

I walked into my bedroom and dialed up Frank's number. He picked up right away.

"Hey Jake, I'm glad you called me back. Rachel has been all through my contacts deleting people. I was able to get your home phone by looking you up."

I didn't even chase why his wife was going through his phone. I learned to stay out of his personal affairs quickly. Instead, I asked, "What's going on, man?"

"First, I need to apologize to you and Tess for the way Rachel acted at dinner. It's a long story, but she thinks I'm having an affair, and there's nothing I can do to convince her that I'm not."

"Well, I hate to ask, but are you?"

"That's just the thing. I'm not cheating. I have been working like crazy on my new job, and she's just not trusting me."

"Okay, man, I believe you. It sounds like you need to take some time out for her and try to make things right," I reasoned.

"Yeah, I do, but I'm just in a lose-lose situation. If I take off from work right now, I could lose my job. Then, we would lose our only income, and she'll probably leave anyway. But hey, that's not why I called. I called because you will never guess who I talked to the other day."

"Who?"

"Your father."

Shock set in as I registered what Frank said.

"What did you just say?" I asked.

"Your father called me out the blue the other day. He thought I was you. I guess Mrs. Sanders thought he was looking for me, but in actuality, it was you he was searching for."

"Well, you can just tell him to get lost," I cut in. "Because I'm not interested in meeting him or hearing from him."

"Jake, your father is James Brockinburg, and he's looking for you. This is major," Frank shrieked.

Brockinburg? So, that's who my sperm donor is?

"You sound super excited about him, Frank. Why don't you just pretend you're his son? It's not like he would know the difference," I said sarcastically.

"Nah. I wouldn't do that, but I thought you might want to get to know your father. I wish mine gave a damn enough to look for me," Frank sounded wounded.

"I just want to know one thing. Why in the hell are you still talking to Ms. Sanders? Those people treated us like shit, man."

"She reached out to me a couple of years ago and apologized for the way the old man treated us. He died of a heart attack, and she wanted me to know he was gone and to apologize to both of us. She said she wishes she had the backbone to stand up to him when we were boys, but she just didn't," Frank said.

"Why didn't she call me?"

"She was afraid to call you. Remember, the day you left you told them both to screw off and to forget they ever knew you."

"I did say that," I admitted as I thought about my father reaching out to Frank. "So, the old man is James Brockinburg. The real estate guru that's all over TV selling dreams?" I asked.

"Yes, that's him. The "How to Beat the Housing Market" guy. And, he sounds like he's sick about taking so long to get to know you. When I answered the phone, he thought I was you, and he immediately started apologizing. He even sounded like he was tearing up."

"Well, he can save the dramatics and pipe dreams for his customers. I don't intend to call him or anything. I appreciate you letting me know though. It was nice hearing from you again, Frank."

"Okay, Jake, but I think you should call him. He sounded like he wanted to get some things off his chest. It's always good to clear the air where the family is concerned," said Frank.

"I think you forget that I don't have a biological family. You and some of the other kids from those homes are my family, and as long as we're good, I'm good," I said.

"Hey, if anyone understands where you're coming from, it's me. Remember, we grew up in those slummy places together. It helped me to find out who the people were that didn't want me. I just thought it might be the same for you, but you don't feel that way, and I respect that," Frank acknowledged.

"I hope you didn't give the asshole my number."

"No, but I told him I would give you his."

"Don't bother."

I heard a baby crying in the distance. Rachel fussed for him to come and help her change the baby's diaper. `

"Alright Jake, I'll catch up with you later."

"Handle your business, man. I'll talk to you soon."

I hung up the phone and sighed. I had no desire to speak with my father, not today, or ever. I made up my mind a long time ago that I didn't need parents. I felt that since I made it this far without them I could make it forever without them.

CHAPTER SIXTEEN

Tess

Jake finished his call and came out of his room looking highly upset.

"Come on, Tess, let's ride to the DA's office," he barked off as an order.

I followed quietly behind him with a brow raised, wondering what happened on this call to put him in such a bad mood. Jake didn't say much of anything the entire ride to the DA's office until I asked what was going on.

"Jake, I noticed you've been quiet since you got that call. Is everything okay?"

"My father called Frank. He wants to meet with me," he spat out.

"Really? Wouldn't that be considered good news?"

"I'm not going to meet him."

"Would you consider giving him a thirty-minute meeting, at least? Maybe somewhere public? You could get answers about why he left you," I suggested.

Jake didn't respond. He gripped the steering wheel and looked as if he was deep in thought.

"I think you should meet him, Jake. But, I would never ask you to do it because I think it's a good idea. It has to be for you," I said.

Jake pulled into the DA's parking lot and turned to me. "It's a definite no."

I sighed, deciding to let it go. I would pick it up later. I had to think of a convincing way to get Jake to be open to meeting his father. I hated knowing he was going through turmoil about it. I got out the car and walked into the tall building holding Jake's hand.

"Welcome to the Fulton County District Attorney's office. How may I help you?" a young lady sitting at the front desk greeted us.

"I'm here to speak with the District Attorney. I have an appointment at 1 p.m.," I answered.

She checked her book for appointments and asked, "Tess Knox?"

"Not for long," Jake murmured soft enough so that only I could hear him.

"Yes, I'm Tess Knox," I answered, glancing at Jake.

He tightened his hold on my hand as the lady directed us to go to the first waiting room.

"I want you to give him his name back as soon as possible," Jake said before our bottoms touched the blue plastic seats.

"I will eventually get around to that. Let me get this trouble of shooting at him off my back first."

Jake chuckled.

"It can wait until that's done, but not a minute longer," he fussed.

"Yes, sir," I teased with a salute.

"Tess Knox," a short, black woman called my name.

Jake rose to walk back with me.

"I need to do this on my own," I told him.

"Are you sure you don't want me to go with you?" he asked.

"Yes, you've done enough already. Let me do this. I got myself into this mess. I should be the one to talk to the DA to try to get out of it," I said.

"Alright. I'll be right out here if you need me," Jake said.

I followed the short lady to the first office on the right. I read the name of the door: Fatima Lattimore, District Attorney. I, instantly, grew nervous. I wasn't about to see the assistant DA or some clerk; I was about to sit down with the district attorney for Fulton County. *I should have let Jake come back here with me.*

Once the door opened, there was no turning back. The woman signaled for me to enter the room.

"Have a seat, Mrs. Knox."

"It's still officially Mrs. Knox, but my name will be changed to my maiden name very soon."

"I'm sure it will. After the damage you did to his office at Lexington, I would say you guys need a lot of space in between you."

"I'm not proud of what I did," I said, gazing away from the DA to look at my twiddling hands. "That's why I'm here. I want to repair any damages and try to start my life over."

"I heard from the officer who took report from Lexington's security lead, and I heard from the owner of Lexington himself. Since the CEO, Mrs. Thompson and Mr. Knox are all willing to give you a break, my office has decided not to press any charges for the shooting. But, we will be requesting anger management courses and reparations for all damages. You will have an official court date where a judge will mandate the courses. Your friend, Jake Weaver, has some pull at the police department. They are the ones that asked me to meet with you to put your mind at east about any jail time for this."

"Oh, thank you, Mrs. Lattimore. I appreciate you meeting with me and giving me a second chance," I said, my voice trembling with excitement.

"You're welcome. But Mrs. Knox, please think before you pull your gun out next time. What you did was reckless, and it could have resulted in someone's death. I know this was a passion-driven shooting, but someone could have died. You don't want that on your conscious. And, I know you don't want to serve time for temporary feelings."

"I know. I regret my behavior that night. At the time, I did wish I had the nerve to shoot one of them. Now, I see how it could have hurt so many people and changed my life forever." *And, I never would have met Jake.*

"The fact that you don't have a record, you have done great volunteer work in the community, and good people have vouched for you is your saving grace. So, let this be a lesson."

"Oh, you don't understand how big of a lesson this all has been for me," I admitted. "Thank you for giving me a second chance," I said.

"Be safe, Tess."

I walked out of the district attorney's office sighing in relief. *I'm not going to jail!*

***

Jake popped a bottle of bubbly to celebrate me being officially free of any charges. "Tonight, I want to toast to my baby, a free woman. Tess doesn't have to worry about wearing those county blues!" he said and lifted his glass to mine.

Tiffany joined us and clinked her glass with ours, then Lou followed suit. We laughed as we finished off our drinks. We had just sat around Jake's round kitchen table and enjoyed a meal of lasagna and salad.

"Thank you! Thank you all so very much. I feel like I should give a speech or something," I began, feeling the light buzz of the wine take over me. "How about I start with, I would like to thank the Fulton County Justice System for allowing me the award of freedom," I said giddily.

Laughter erupted around the table.

"No, let me get serious. I'm truly blessed to have met such a great man who lifted me out of a rut. I don't know what I would have done had he not showed up in Gulf Shores. You're the best, Jake."

"That makes two of us who are blessed by him," Tiffany interjected. "He thought enough of us to put his neck on the line and help us out of our situations." Tiffany and I smiled at Jake. "If it wasn't for him, I never would have met Lou," she added. Her and Lou had a beautiful moment of staring into each other's eyes smiling.

"Yes, Jake really is all of that," I said and winked at him.

He cleared his throat. He looked visibly disturbed by the way I stared at him as if he was a drop of water in the desert. Jake stood and spoke to Tiffany.

"Do you mind putting the dishes away?" he asked her.

"Not at all," she replied.

"I'll help her," Lou added.

"Tess, to the back," he said as if he'd summoned me into his office for doing something wrong.

"What'd I do?" I asked, following behind Jake confused.

As soon as we reached his room, he slammed the door shut and towered over me.

"Why do you look at me like that in front of people? Do you have any clue of what it does to me?" he asked as he pulled me firmly into his arms.

"Does it cause the big imprint pressed against my stomach?" I asked in a low, teasing tone.

"I see you like teasing me. Turn around."

"Huh?"

"I said, turn around."

I turned around facing the bedroom door. I heard Jake unzipping his pants. He pressed me into the door and slipped his hand up my backside. His tongue slid over the hot skin of my neck as he lifted my skirt and moved his thumbs into the edges of my panties. Jake slid my panties to the floor with ease. My heart pounded vibrantly in my chest as he kissed his way from the backs of my knees to my neck again. I let out a series of sweet moans as he took his time to cherish my body.

Jakes manhood rested against my ass as he held me exactly where he wanted me. He propped my legs open with the weight of his knee, spreading my legs far apart. I braced myself as the tip of his rod pressed against my opening. I whimpered as his engorged head thrust inside my pussy lips. A ferocious moan escaped me. I tried unsuccessfully to grab ahold of the door.

"Ouwee!" I screamed as my walls grabbed onto his hard shaft and pulled him inside. My cry echoed in the bedroom, and I knew I could be heard throughout the house.

Jake picked up speed, pounding into me. Every time he connected with my walls, my breasts bounced freely. He reached up and grabbed them both into his hands, rolling the nipples in between his fingers.

"Damn baby…you are too hot, too tight," he mumbled his pleasures against my ear as he pounded into me relentlessly.

My breath caught every time his balls reached my nether lips. I could feel myself starting to shake. I was about to lose control of my legs.

Jake wrapped around me like a blanket. He was all over me as I sheathed him like a glove. We fit perfectly. He fucked me to new heights and eased out of me to spray his cum all over my plump ass cheeks. My body pulsated for minutes after he left me.

*

On our third round, we were lying in bed. This time, I was the one licking the tip of his manhood, teasing him with my mouth before taking Jake all into my throat. I had him right where I wanted him. He was about to blow. Then, I stopped and sat up. I looked into his hungry eyes that were trained on me.

"I want you to call your father," I purred.

"Really, baby? Right now is not the time to bring images of that fucker into my head."

I licked the tip of his manhood again, sucking him back into my mouth before I withdrew again.

"I really think you should…"

"Tess, come on, baby. Don't do this."

"I want you to, baby," I said as I kissed from his balls, up his shaft, and to the head where I kissed him passionately.

"Oh, damn."

"Are you going to call?" I asked coyly.

"Alright. I'll call the fucker. I will call him tonight, just cover me back up, baby." Jake's fingers entangled into my hair and pushed my head back down on his engorged head down to the shaft. He stroked my mouth until the marvelous taste of his cum filled my mouth and rushed down my throat. "Fuck yeah!" he roared, and I smiled as he fought to gather his senses. "That was amazing! You're more than I ever imagined you would be, Tess," he said as he fell back on the bed completely spent.

I laid down beside him feeling good. Mission accomplished.

CHAPTER SEVENTEEN

Jake

A few days later, I watched my baby climb into my Corvette and ride off to go shopping for clothes. I went back into the house, sat on the sofa, and began flipping through channels on the TV. I had found something good to watch when my phone rang.

"Hello," I picked up without checking the caller ID.

"Hi, Son," a gravelly voice said.

"Who is this?"

"It's James Brockinburg, your father."

I knew this moment would come. In fact, I promised Tess I would call him, but I didn't plan for it to happen this soon. Now that he was on my phone, I wanted to take my promise back. Brockinburg was the last man on earth I wanted to hear from.

"What do you want?" I asked.

"Well, for starters I'd like to meet you. I have a lot that I need to tell you and only a little time to say it," he said.

"Let me ask you something. Why would I want to meet you after making it this far in life? What's the point of us meeting now?" I was curious as to how he would answer those questions.

"I'm sorry for not being there for you, Son. It wasn't right," he replied.

"But you didn't answer my question. Why should we meet now when we've done just fine without each other this long?"

"Because I missed out on so much already. You deserve more than what I gave, and I know that now. I want to work on the things I did wrong," he said.

"Oh, that's how you feel, Brockinburg? You, with all of your money and high-society living, you're sorry for not being there for little ole' me? I guess being sorry now makes it alright," I chastised him with an evil tone bellowing over the phone line.

"Listen—"

"No, you listen. You run around the country putting on televised schemes about how people can get rich if they only give you a couple thousand of their hard earned dollars for training. You yell at the top of your lungs at these people about how you can change their lives, then when you get on the phone with me, a son you have neglected for twenty-seven years, all you can say is 'I'm sorry for not being there?' You know what? Fuck you! Don't ever call me your son again."

"Son, I—"

I swiped my phone off to end the call. I told Tess I would talk to him and I did. I just couldn't listen to any more of his BS. I wondered how he got my cell phone number. I hoped Frank didn't overstep his boundaries and give it to him, but it wasn't like I was insulated with my bail bonding business attached to my phone. He could have gotten it anywhere. I made a note to have Lou change all of my numbers. I didn't want that fucker ever to call me again.

My doorbell rang. I opened the door expecting to see Tess. Instead, it was Brockinburg, the real estate mogul, in the flesh. He wore an expensive gray suit, loafers and a stoic look on his oval, overly tanned face. He was my height, and I could see how we resembled in some ways.

"Wow, you just don't get it, do you?" I asked. "I don't want to see you!"

"I knew you would hang up on me, Son," he said, walking past me as if his name was on the lease. The man some called my father was clearly in his golden years. He reeked of money, power and influence. "I know I'm intruding, but this is of grave importance. I don't have much time, so I will get straight to the point. Over the years, I have amassed a large amount of wealth, a little over a billion dollars." He looked at me, waiting on my response.

I was sure he thought talking about his money would impress me. Instead, it made me want to toss him out on his face.

"I don't care about your money. It means nothing here," I yelled, my neck muscles flexing as I stepped into his face. The spittle from my words hit his face as I barked at him. "I don't need you or your money!"

He didn't budge. He simply began to tell a story.

"In my whole life, I never wanted kids. I told every woman I ever dated to make sure they had good birth control, because I didn't want any children. Then, I met your mother. We had a whirlwind affair. I was very fond of her. I couldn't get enough of that woman. Then, she got pregnant. She had forgotten to take her birth control, and I thought she was purposely trying to force me to settle down with her. She thought I was seeing other women, but after we got together, I never touched another woman. All I wanted was Jacquelyn."

"So, that was her name?" I asked.

"Yes, and she was beautiful. I just didn't think I could live up to the responsibility of being a father. When I rejected her pregnancy, she ran off, and I never heard from her again. I could have searched for you, Son. I could have done more. I just threw myself into my work and let the both of you slip to the back of my mind. Yet, every day I thought about you. Every day, I had you into the back of my mind. I figured you were in better hands than being with a man as damaged as I was."

"I wasn't in good hands, Brockinburg. Far from it. The places I've been and the people I've seen, no child should ever have to deal with."

"I'm so sorry, Son. I wish I were a better man."

"What do you want from me Brockinburg...a prize for admitting you're a deadbeat?"

"I never should have let your mother walk out of my life. I never should have walked away from you."

"Well, she walked out of both of our lives, so there that."

"Son, I'm sorry about the past."

"I don't like to dwell on the past, which is why I think you being here is pointless," I said.

"Look, Son, I didn't get this far along in my life being naïve. I know we'll never play catch or have a normal father-son relationship. What I want to do for you now is give you all that I have. I want to make you heir to all of my businesses. Basically, you are the heir to my vast fortune," he said. The mention of his money came with an air of smugness. Yet, his money couldn't erase Old Man Sanders and all of the horrible places I lived in as a child away from my memories.

"I wouldn't accept a dime from you or any man like you. Do you hear me? Not one dime!" I stalked to the door. "I don't want anything to do with you. Now, get out."

I flung the door open, and Tess stood on the other side with a bag in one hand and the other raised to knock.

"Uh, hey," she said.

I was sure the scowl on my face was the reason she stood there with her mouth hanging open in bafflement.

"Hey, babe. Never mind the old man. He was just leaving."

"Yes, I was about to leave, young lady," Brockinburg said to Tess. Then, he turned back to me. "I hope you'll think about what I said. Because whether you accept it or not, as my only child, it will always be yours." He placed an envelope on the foyer table before walking out the door.

"That was your father?" Tess asked once we were alone.

"Yeah, and I'm glad he's gone. He had some nerve walking in here thinking that I want his money."

"Wait. What happened?"

"He called and we talked. I basically told him I didn't want to hear from him again. Then, he knocked on the door as if he was already outside when he called."

"Wow, so he's really trying to reach out."

"Yes, but I'm not interested in anything he has to offer. I believe in leaving the past in the past, Tess. You have to understand that about me," I said.

"What is this?" Tess asked of the envelope on the table.

"Trash," I responded.

My phone rang before I could toss it out. I looked at the caller ID and didn't recognize the number. Thinking it was Brockinburg again, I growled into the phone like a madman. "Didn't I tell you to leave me the fuck alone?"

"Jake?" the woman on the other end said quizzically.

"Who is this?"

"This is Rachel."

"Frank's Rachel?" I asked, confused as to why she would be calling me.

The mention of her name brought Tess's attention to my call.

"Yes, I know you're probably surprised that I'm calling, but I'm giving Frank a surprise birthday party in Atlanta next weekend. It's only going to be some of his closest friends, so it would be great if you could come."

"Oh, sure. Text me the details, and I'm there for my boy. Do you need me to bring anything?" I asked.

"Lovely. No, just bring yourself, and that will be more than enough," she said in a haughty tone. "I'll send everything over to you now. See you soon, Jake," Rachel said before hanging up.

Tess grabbed my hand and walked me over to the couch. She pushed me onto the sofa and sat on my lap.

"Okay Jake, tell me what the hell is going on," she demanded.

I told her everything that happened while she was out shopping.

"Jake, you will get through this," she said, kissing me.

"As long as I have you, I'll make it through anything," I replied, hugging Tess tightly. It felt good to receive her love. It was something I never wanted to stop.

***

One Week Later

I sat in the private lounge at the Hilton Downtown thinking about the large lump sum of money my father was ready to deposit into my banking account, along with the billions in assets available to be transferred to my control. I never imagined I'd be stuck with a dilemma of whether I'd live my days out as the wealthiest man in Atlanta or continue my life helping one person beat the justice system at a time.

You can do both. That's what Tess told me, and it sounded tempting. Only because I'd do anything to give her the best this world has to offer. With that money, I would be able to help more people get their lives back on track.

I sat in the lounge, waiting on Frank and the other guests to arrive at his surprise birthday party. Rachel told me when I got there the other guests were due to arrive at any minute. But the longer I sat there waiting, the more impatient I became. Sitting in that room alone gave me too much time to think about Brockinburg and his unwanted entrance into my life.

I looked at my watch. Tess would be there soon. She had a meeting with a potential business partner. Since she hadn't worked since before she married Amiri, I encouraged her to lay the groundwork for starting a new tax office. For the past few weeks, I'd watched her go from broken to ready to take over the world. I wanted my woman to be all she could be when it came to her career, life and especially romantically.

As I sat at the table thinking about the moment she would arrive, I felt my body come alive. Two tiny hands slid down the front of my blazer headed toward my stomach, and I smiled. The touch wasn't as soft as Tess's, but I knew like hell it had to be her. No one else would touch me like that.

When I crooked my neck to look at the tiny hands, I jumped up out of my seat. Standing eye to eye with Frank's wife, I yelled, "What are you doing, Rachel?" I backed away from her, looking at her like she was the green-eyed monster.

Unfazed by my response to her, she sauntered toward me with a determined look on her flawless face.

"Rachel, what the fuck is your problem?"

"Oh, Jake, stop playing coy. You know I want you," she said matter-of-factly. "You should have picked up on that the first night we met."

"But, you're my friend's wife."

"And…"

"And, you don't know me like that."

"I know enough to know what I want."

"But, Frank is on the way." I kept tossing out scenarios, hoping one of them would rattle some senses into this woman.

"Oh, Frank isn't in Atlanta. No one is coming here tonight but us."

"Tess is coming. I invited her. She should be here any moment." I looked at the doorway.

Rachel stepped closer to me and invaded my space.

"Get rid of her. I can make you forget all about her, just watch and see." She got close enough to touch me, and I pushed her away.

"You are crazy out of your mind if you think I'm going to touch you. I love my woman more than I like you. And Frank, wait until he hears this shit."

"He'll never believe you, so don't waste your breath. I have ways of making Frank believe whatever I tell him," she said confidently.

"We'll see about that," I threatened as I backed up toward the exit.

She sashayed toward me with a prowling look in her green eyes.

"Jake, be real. You knew when you got here there was no party, but you hung around because you want this as much as me." She slid her tongue across her red lipstick and stalked toward me again.

I continued to back away.

"Rachel, I don't know what the hell kind of person you are, but I suggest you stay away from me. I would never do my friend like that. And, I'd never cheat on Tess." I hoped talking to her would put some sense into her head and help her remember she was a married woman, married to my friend no less.

The woman didn't hear a word I said. As I walked out of the room, she continued to pursue me.

"Stop acting like a lunatic, Rachel," I warned her. I pushed her slightly so that she wouldn't press her body against me as she followed me.

She stumbled back losing her balance. I reached for her to make sure she didn't fall. While my arms wrapped around her to catch her, she clung to me and kissed my lips. A loud gasp and squeaking sound brought my attention to the entrance. The hurt look on Tess's face crushed me.

"Tess, baby, this is not what it looks like," I said as rage rose inside of me.

Rachel would be on the receiving end of more than what she bargained for if I lost Tess.

CHAPTER EIGHTEEN

Tess

People were always trying to make me go postal, but a tiny voice deep within kept nagging at me, pleading even, for me to not believe my eyes this time. "What's going on in here?" I asked with as much calm as I could muster.

"You have eyes. What does it look like?" Rachel said, touching her lips and looking at Jake with a smile.

"Tess, Rachel kissed me when I was trying to break her fall," Jake said, turning to Rachel. "You can believe I'm calling Frank as soon as I leave here to let him know you came on to me. That man is my best friend. How dare you try to come between us like that?" Jake looked disgusted. His broad face turned up into a frown. His muscles kept flexing, which was a tell that Jake was highly upset.

Rachel humped her shoulders as if she was unbothered by anything.

"I don't care. Go ahead and call him. It's not like he gives a damn about what I do," she said.

"Oh, I see what you're trying to do. You're trying to get your husband's attention," I surmised. "But you see, I do give a damn about what you do with my man," I said, claiming Jake and stepping into Rachel's space. "As long as you live, don't you lay a finger on him. Do you hear me?"

"So, you're just going to pretend you didn't see him kiss me?" Rachel asked with a smirk that begged to be slapped away.

"You'd better be glad I'm a changed woman." I had to start my anger management classes next week, and I wasn't trying to end up in jail. "Jake, I'm leaving out of here before I lose it on her."

"What are you going to do, fight me like a hood girl?" Rachel said, sounding ridiculous.

This woman obviously knew nothing about me. Thank God there were no guns nearby. When I turned around to head back in her direction, Jake grabbed me around the waist and picked me up.

"I'll show you a hood girl!" I yelled as Jake carried me out of the building.

"Tess, I need you to calm down. You already have enough to deal with," Jake whispered close to my ear. "Don't do this."

His hot breath against my skin settled me. He invaded the space around me with his massive physique and woodsy cologne filling all the air. Once he put me down, I turned to him.

"Jake, why were you kissing her?"

He looked surprised at my question.

"I didn't kiss her. I would never kiss another woman. She came on to me, and I was backing away from her. I pushed her, and she pretended to fall, so I tried to catch her. That's when she snuck a kiss on my lips, and you walked in."

"That bitch is so trifling. I knew that much the day I met her," I admitted.

"I know, you warned me about her then. I didn't want to believe she was doing Frank like that. I should have never come here without you, but I thought it was going to be a crowd of people here," Jake explained. "It was a setup," he added.

The way he had his arms wrapped around Rachel reminded me of a Marissa and Amiri situation happening all over again. There was one thing I wasn't willing to be ever again in life, and that was a fool. No way. I promised myself that the first time a man I was involved with appeared to want another woman I would let him go. It didn't matter that Jake had my heart hogtied up and strapped down to his. I refused to be his fool, just as much as I refused to be Amiri's, whom I also thought held my heart at one point. But alas, I knew Jake told the truth. Rachel was a wolf in sheep's clothing, and her sheep clothing was scant.

"Jake, I believe you. I don't think you touched that woman. I believe she would do anything to make other people as miserable as she is," I said sincerely.

The grief left Jake's face with my admittance. He grabbed me up into his arms and held me tight.

"Thank you, baby. I hope you know I would never mistreat you. I'll never hurt you like that. I love you, Tess!"

With me still in his arms, Jake walked over to his car. He sat me inside his car and ran around to get in the driver's seat.

"What's on your mind?" he asked, once he slid behind the wheel.

"Jake, let's just get out of here. I don't want to be here," I said, feeling like I wanted to go home and lay inside his arms for the rest of the night.

The fact that I'd mentally referred to his house as my home didn't escape me. I did feel at home with Jake. A part of me hoped it was something that would stand the test of time *and* other women.

Jake started the ignition and drove to his house. As soon as we entered the door, he dragged me down the hall to his room and fell onto the bed, pulling me along with him.

"Let's cuddle," I said, wrapping my arms around his waist.

"Oh, we're going to cuddle alright. My work is cut out for me in getting you to understand that you're the only one for me."

He took both of my hands in his a dragged them above my head. He held me down against the bed as if I weighed nothing. He subdued me with such ease. I didn't have enough energy in my body to push him off. How in the hell did we even get to the bedroom? It was all a blur. I didn't remember him pushing me toward the room, pinning my hands down, or pressing his nose against mine so that we were eye to eye.

"Jake—" I began, but he cut me off.

"Listen to me. I haven't seen the beauty of another woman since I laid eyes on you. You are all that I want, all that I will ever want," he said.

The look in his eyes shook my soul. His breath was so close to mine that I had no choice but to breathe in his words. I felt his soul bleeding into mine as his breath entered my mouth.

"Jake, you're everything," I admitted as the gates of my heart burst open allowing him in entirely. My body became his as pangs of passion shoot straight to my womanhood.

"And, you are mine," he said.

"I trust you completely," I assured him. I hoped I wasn't being a fool for love, once again.

Jake slid down my pants and panties together. He tore open my blouse and released a nipple from my lace bra. He suckled on the hard nipple, bringing me intense pleasure. He then tore his clothes away from his body and tossed them in a heap on the floor. His manhood pulsated against my entrance. We were both anxious to be one again, as we would always be.

CHAPTER NINETEEN
Jake

Six Months Later

The mess with Frank didn't go over well. When I called to tell him what happened, he broke down and vented his frustrations over how many times she'd cheated on him since they got married. She'd cheated on him six times already, well seven if he included her coming on to me. He said he did so much to make her happy, but she cheated anyway. Frank was at his wit's end. The only reason he was hanging on was because of their child. It was difficult to be the one to break the news to him about her kissing me, but I had to do it.

"I think you should divorce her," was my advice to him. *"But I wouldn't judge you if you stayed to work on your marriage,"* I included.

I didn't know what else to say. Most of all, I wanted to relay to Frank that I never wanted to be put in a vulnerable position to be around Rachel again. My relationship with Tess meant too much to me than to risk it for any woman, my friend's wife or not. Tess had started her anger management classes. I didn't want to risk her freedom because Frank's wife was disrespectful to us continually. I also didn't want any bad blood between me and Frank. He told me he understood where I was coming from. We ended our conversation on a good note, talking about football. That was six months ago.

Today, I sat at my desk at work thinking about Tess. When I met her, her spirit was broken. Now, there's not a moment she's not smiling or speaking encouragement to someone. She'd developed a great relationship with Tiffany and showed her so many things, including different careers she could work, helping her with baby Aniya, and being an all-around good role model for Tiffany.

She hadn't mentioned Amiri or Marissa one time in the past few months, which was always a plus. The fact that I lived on the outskirts of Atlanta in Duluth, and her new tax office was in Duluth, cut down the chances of either of us bumping into them. I insisted all of her numbers be changed, so the past could stay where it was meant to be, the past.

There was one thing Tess wouldn't leave in the past. My beautiful girlfriend, who now was pregnant with my child, twisted my arm to do something I never thought I'd do in a million years—invite my sperm donor to dinner. I half didn't expect him to accept, but when his secretary called to confirm he would be there, I knew then I was stuck with this dinner. I told Frank about it, and he was glad to hear I agreed to meet with Brockinburg. He sent his best wishes.

I felt the tiniest twinge of hope over hooking up with my father, but I felt bad for Frank. He wanted to make it work with Rachel. He had done so much dirt to other women, only to finally give his heart and last name away to a woman who treated him like dirt. I guess people are right when they say Karma is real.

Earlier this morning, which was six months after the incident with Rachel, Frank sent a picture of him standing in front of a divorce lawyer's office. Along with the image, he sent a long message telling me how her crossing the line with me, his friend, was the last straw. It had been something she couldn't live down with him. He never got over it.

Good for you, man, I texted back. I was glad he took a stand for his dignity. I would never tell him, but Rachel was rotten to the core. He could do so much better than her.

Just as I finished up that text, Tiffany came by the office to tell me she'd found her a new job and a place about an hour away. But that wasn't the kicker. Lou stood next to her as she made that announcement.

"So, are you two dating or something?" I asked though I knew the answer. Then, it hit me. Lou commuted an hour to work each day. Tiffany said she was moving an hour away. "Wait, are you moving in with Lou?" I asked Tiffany, then turned to Lou. "What's going on, LuKane?"

"Yes, and yes to both of your questions," he answered as he took her hand in his protectively. "I'm going to take good care of her and the baby, too," Lou said with pride as they looked at each other.

Over the past months, Lou had settled down a lot. He got extra close with Tiffany and her baby. I hadn't heard one peep about Joogie. As I looked at Lou with Tiffany, I could only imagine what he had done to make that happen. Knowing him, he'd probably spent the last six months taking Joogie's squad out one man at a time. Meanwhile, Joogie would be in jail for a long time.

"Well, alright man. Congratulations to you two. You didn't have to be so secretive," I said. They had been discreet, but it was obvious they had a thing for each other. I just didn't know they'd taken it this far.

"We weren't trying to say anything until we were serious. Now, we are," Tiffany said, "...thank you for everything, Jake," she added as she rushed to my desk to hug my neck.

Then, Tiffany ran back over to retake Lou's hand.

"Catch you later, boss man," Lou said as he walked out with Tiffany hand in hand.

"So, you're just not going to work today?" I asked Lou.

"I'll be back in later," he replied.

Wow. I sat there shocked by my eventful the morning, and it was only ten a.m.

CHAPTER TWENTY

Tess

I had to pick up a few things for dinner. Jake's father was coming over, and I wanted everything to be perfect. I put the car in park and looked up at the grocery store. It looked packed as hell in there. My buzzing cell dragged my attention away from the crowd. Marissa's number displayed across the screen. I didn't have it programmed into my phone, but I remembered it by heart. My first thought was to ignore the call and send her to voicemail, but something inside of me wanted to hear from her.

"How did you get my number?" I asked as my greeting.

"Hey Tess," she replied, and then the line went silent.

"Well, how did you get my number, and what did you call me for?" I asked impatiently.

"I got it from someone at your new office. I just wanted you to know that I love you," she said softly.

"Marissa, please don't start that. I've had enough of the fake love from you and Amiri to last a lifetime. I'm in a good place now, so there's no need to drag me back to where we were months ago."

"No, hear me out. I do feel horrible for everything, really horrible." She paused. "Listen, I know we'll never be friends again, and that's not why I called."

"Then, why did you call?" I asked, my patience running thin.

"I called because I want you to know my side of the story. You've summed me up as a homewrecking bitch that didn't value our friendship, and on the surface, that's what it seems. But, if you took a minute to dig deeper, you'd know I only wanted the best for you. I wanted it so badly that I sacrificed my happiness for yours," she whined.

"What the hell does that even mean, when you're the one that screwed my husband, Marissa?" I asked.

I had already found out that Marissa's baby wasn't Amiri's. He came to my office a month ago sobbing like he just received a death sentence. I thought Marissa told him he contracted a terminal illness by the way he acted. That's how hurt Amiri was. When he told me her baby wasn't his, I didn't know what to say to him. A tiny piece of me felt sorry for Amiri. But, the unforgiving part of me politely asked him to leave after he poured his heart out. I hadn't told Jake about Amiri's little visit because I didn't want Jake to lose it. My mind rushed to a thousand places. None of those places were where I needed to go, which was inside that store to get my items for dinner.

"So, let me tell you the real story, Tess," Marissa's voice cut through my thoughts. "Amiri and I had a crush on each other before you got married. I sold accounting services to his office. Every time I went in there, I would try to see him to make conversation. We used to flirt with each other a little. Then, I would leave, and that was the extent of it."

"So, why didn't you get with him yourself instead of setting me up on a blind date with him?" I asked.

"Because at the time, I was seeing someone, and you didn't have anyone."

"So, that day I told you I needed to start dating again, and you suggested this guy you knew, you knew then that you also had been flirting with him? I don't understand, Marissa. Your explanation isn't making this any better," I told her as I grew annoyed.

"I didn't know you'd end up marrying him," she said in a dry tone. "When you guys started getting serious, I didn't know how to come clean about my feelings. You were in love with him, and I simply didn't know what to do."

"Well, you should have given me a heads up that you were fucking him too!" I retorted. "That would have been a start."

"The sex didn't come until later. At first, I tried very hard to keep my attraction for Amiri at bay, and he did too. It wasn't until that morning he came over to change my tire so that I could go to work. It was raining. After he finished putting the tire on, he came inside my apartment to dry off and put on another t-shirt that I had in the closet."

"So, knowing he was my man, you invited him into your apartment to change t-shirts...go on."

"I just didn't want him to get sick. It was cold out."

"And by riding his dick, I'm sure you warmed him right on up. That's as effective as a cough drop from what I hear. You know what, why am I on this phone with you?"

"Look, I tried to sacrifice what I felt for him so that you could be happy. It was wrong the way I handled it, but I did think I was doing something good at the time. That day, when he came over to my house, everything we had been avoiding couldn't be avoided any longer. We couldn't resist our attraction. We promised not to do it ever again, and we didn't until...until—"

"Until what, Marissa!" I snapped at her.

"Until your wedding night. Seeing you standing there, dressed and ready to marry Amiri unraveled something in my sensibility. It drove me insane to know I had no one, and the man I was attracted to the most was about to be yours. So, I did the wrong thing. I cornered him at the reception and reminded him of what we had. I told him I'd be waiting for him at the W that night. I went with the wrong emotions, and I lost you. I got the man but lost my heart."

I started to laugh. Then, I was laughing uncontrollably. No matter what, the man Marissa sounded proud to have would come back to me at any moment if I wanted him, but I didn't. What worse punishment for her than to know her man would sleep with another woman on his wedding night? In her heart of hearts, she had to know he was no good.

"Well, thanks for calling me to clear that up, Marissa, but at the end of the day, we're at the same place we started. I can only wish other women give you the same courtesies in your love life that gave to me," I said, hanging up the phone.

Though I would never forget, I hoped that one day I would forgive her completely. I just wasn't there yet.

CHAPTER TWENTY ONE

Jake

The rest of the week flew by. Saturday was there before I knew it. The day had come to sit at the same dinner table as Brockinburg. I never thought I would break bread with my father, but Tess outdid herself. She prepared grilled steaks, sautéed vegetables, and baked sweet potatoes. Her culinary skills were the only high point about the night. I loved seeing my woman throw down in the kitchen. Man, did it smell delicious.

This dinner was going to be interesting. It would take everything in me to get through it without snapping. I had to show my sperm donor I was just fine without him. I needed to show him for me, more than for him. It's not like I wanted it to be this way. Me hating my father. I would have preferred to have a real man step up and do his job of raising his son. Instead, I had a coward that ran and hid behind his money and power. What could he possibly want from me now?

I used to dream I'd kill him. That way, he could really be dead to me. I would never want to cause anyone the type of pain he created for me. The baby I put in Tess's stomach (and I made sure to put one there) would have nothing to worry about in this world. Not if I could help it.

"Hey, sweetheart. You got it smelling good in here. Why do you have to cook like this for my sperm donor? You could have cooked this for me," I said to Tess as I snaked my arms around her waist and hugged her close to my body. Her baby bump was so small that I could hardly feel it, but I loved rubbing her stomach anyway. Knowing my baby was growing inside of her gave me everything I needed as a man.

"Don't start, Jake. You promised to be nice tonight."

"But, you smell so damn good. Why don't we call off this dinner, and I drop to my knees and eat you right here in this kitchen?" I whispered close to my baby's ear.

"Jake! Stop being so freaky. I have to finish this up."

"That's what I'm saying. I can call him right quick and tell him to stay where he is. Then, I'll eat you up and try some of your food next."

Tess ground her plump bottom into my crotch, and that was her tell that she needed me as much as I needed her.

"I was just about to go get in the shower before your father gets here. I'll leave the door open for you if you need one too." She walked toward my bedroom swinging her apple shaped bottom from side to side, and it hypnotized me.

My head swayed to her rhythm as I followed behind her like a fucking puppy. I trekked into the bathroom, unbuttoning my pants as I walked.

"Thank you, baby," I said in a low, gravelly tone. My hands clamped down on her shoulders as I stood behind her and massaged her shoulders.

"For what? Giving you sex all the damn time?"

"No." I closed my eyes and bit back a groan as she rotated her ass against my now naked crotch. I could already feel her slickness on my manhood as if I was inside her. I spun her around and gripped her backside firmly in my hands. "Thank you for forcing me to do what I never would have done alone."

She looked me square in the eyes and deep feelings of mutual appreciation stared back at me.

"You came into my life when I was at my lowest," she said in an alluring tone that enraptured me inside of her world. "Within a matter of months, you have made me feel so alive, so wanted, and needed. You have done more to help me than I could ever express. It's only right that I push you to do something that might give you closure and hopefully open the door to a relationship with your father, something I could only dream of having again," she said.

Tess was referring to the dreams she had where her father would come to speak with her. A day didn't go by when she didn't talk about her parents and wanting to be connected with them again. That was the reason she pushed so hard for me to build a relationship with my father.

"I wouldn't go so far as to say we'll have a relationship, but I get what you're saying, baby," I muttered near her ear as I bit down on her earlobe. I was done talking. I breathed in her exotic scent, and my manhood swelled with anticipation of becoming one with what's mine. "I want you naked now."

I stepped back to watch her strip out of her oversized t-shirt and pants.

"Jake, our company will be here in less than an hour. We really do need to make this shower quick so that we can get dressed. I still need to finish setting up the table," she said in a raspy voice. Another sign she was dying for me to be buried deep inside of her.

"I'm going to take care of us first. Everyone else can wait," I groaned.

When she bent down to take off her panties, I pressed my hardness against the split of her ass. She moved away and stepped into the shower.

"Come on in, caveman."

She looked back at me and giggled.

I stepped into the shower with her, took the soapy bath sponge from her hand, and laid it aside. I grasped her slick body and pulled her close to me. My head swooped down to capture her lips. My hands swept over every inch of her smooth, hot flesh as I pulled her as close to me as possible with her small baby bump between us.

Tess's moans broke me. I picked her up, and she wrapped her legs around my waist. My hardness rested against her slick entrance before I thrust upward, reuniting us in our most perfect union by sheathing my manhood with her tight, gushy center. She closed her eyes and moaned out my name. The sound alone made me give her my all.

"Open your eyes, baby. I want you to look at me when I make love to you," I growled against her ear as I tattooed my name all over her.

"I'm looking at you," she murmured, barely able to speak.

I plunged into her heat over and over again, biting down on my bottom lip as I tried not to explode before she reached her climax with me. When Tess started to tremble, I knew I could let go. I rammed into her core, filling her up with love with each blow.

"Marry...me," I breathed out between each stroke. I had no intention of asking her like this, but it's what came to mind as I erupted.

"Yes! Yes! Yes!" she said as a wave of orgasm devoured her being. A loud moan escaped her lips and was captured by mine.

I never in my life felt a tighter bond with anyone. It was time she became mine officially.

****

The shower lasted longer than either of us planned. We had to rush into our clothes before my father arrived. The doorbell chimed just as we finished getting dressed. I walked out to answer the door.

"Hey," I said as my greeting to Brockinburg.

"Hi Jake, thanks for inviting me," he said, walking in. In his hand was a bottle of wine. He held it out to me, but I didn't take it.

"I thought I told you that you didn't have to bring anything," I said.

Tess came up beside me and interjected.

"I'll put that way. Welcome to our home, Mr. Brockinburg," Tess said.

The words "our home" did something to me every time she said it. It gave me a sense of pride and caused me to lighten up toward my father, if only for a little while.

"Thank you for the kind welcome, Tess," Brockinburg said, "...but please, call me James."

Tess giggled.

"I'll do that, James," she said.

"Come on in. Tess has cooked a great dinner. Let's go eat before it gets cold," I said, turning and walking toward the kitchen. I had every intention of getting this little dinner over as fast as possible. The sooner it started, the better.

"Jake, I'll just be a minute. Why don't you and your father sit in the living room for a while I fix the table?" she said and gave me a nod.

"Sure," I said, but the look I gave her let her know she would be paying for intentionally trying to make me talk to my father. Yeah, she would pay for that quick one all night long.

I walked Brockinburg into the living room. We took a seat, and, for the remainder of the evening, I couldn't believe how easy the conversation flowed between him, Tess and me. He talked a lot about his businesses. I listened most of the time intently. Other times, I told him about the bail bonding business I started. That much we had in common. Beyond that, we had a lot to fill in.

After dinner, we found ourselves back in the living room talking.

"Dinner was delicious! That girl can cook. You'd better keep her," Brockinburg said to me as he pointed to Tess. "Or better yet, I should be trying to see if I could take her home with me," he teased.

"No, I don't share what's mine," I said seriously.

"I understand that," he said, smiling at Tess. "I never liked to share either, so that's one trait you picked up from your father."

"I guess so," I said in a low tone.

"Jake, there's one more thing I need to tell you about flipping property," Brockinburg began another lesson about property. It was starting to feel as if his sole reason for coming to dinner was to unload all of his business sense onto me at once. He finished talking about flipping property and was about to start talking about equity when I interrupted.

"How did you do it?"

"Oh, flipping houses are as easy as taking candy from a baby. My first one, I got a small loan from a bank and took a gamble on a little three bedroom in Lithonia. I got a thirty thousand dollar profit from it. I was like 'oh my God.' I was able to pay the loan back and everything. Walked away with thirty thousand for one month's work. After that, I was in it for life," he gushed with joy.

"I'm not talking about real estate," I said sounding frustrated. "I'm talking about throwing my mom away and acting like you didn't have a child. Tell me how you did *that*? How could you walk around for seventy-six years and pretend like no one carried your blood, like there was no young man you should have been teaching all of this shit years ago? I'm just curious!" I fumed.

Tess touched my hand. I covered her hand in mine to let her know I was okay. This had to be said. I expected the old man to talk about what mattered to me.

"Jake, I didn't come here with excuses or empty apologies. I've lived a very successful life in business, but I've done some lousy things as a man. Denying my only son is the worst thing I've done," he admitted with hurt in his voice as he stared me in the eye. His eyes begged for an apology and for acceptance.

And, there he was. Brockinburg, the man. That's who I wanted to talk to. Not the fucking real estate guy.

"That's the one thing you've said tonight that makes sense to me," I told him. "And, I appreciate that. Because, you see, this woman right here." I raised Tess's hand that was inside of mine. "She's carrying my first child. Even with my child not being in the world yet, I bend over and kiss this little body that's growing in her stomach. I love this woman with everything I have inside of my soul, but the love I have for the child growing inside of her is unexplainable."

Brockinburg sat back in the chair as if all the wind had left his lungs. His mouth hung open with words seemingly unable to escape.

"You're a better man than I could ever dream of being," he said finally. "My pride has always been in my money and power. I spent decades making money and boasting about it. It wasn't until recently when I sat in my multi-million dollar mansion and looked around at the many things I own, some I can't even pronounce, that I realized just how miserable I am. Alone and miserable, I might add. I regret running your mother away, but to be honest, I was not a good man to anyone at the time, and I was wrong. I'm happy it didn't take you decades to realize a dollar can't hold you, it can't talk to you, it can't console you when you're sick, and it damn sure can't make you a good person."

"Well, I'm glad to hear you say these things. I'm also glad we got a chance to talk," I said, standing up to see him out.

"Will you take a seat at the head of my real estate empire, Jake?" he asked, sounding hopeful. "I want you to have it all. Though I must forewarn you that you will instantly become a billionaire, and that comes with some challenges. People will come out of the woodworks trying to get a piece of your newfound fortune. They will try to vulture off you. They will even make up media stories about you, simply because you have money. I have no doubt that you will be able to handle whatever comes your way. You are tough as nails just like your mother."

For the very first time in my adult life, the mention of my mother tugged at my heart. Getting to know her was a longing I had suppressed. A longing I never planned to fulfil. Yet, as Brockingburg brought her up, I felt a need deep within to meet her. I also felt the need to accept what he was offering for her sake. Because of her wanting to be in the presence of a rich man years ago, and being rejected by the same man, I would take his fortune as a right that should have been afforded to my mother.

"Yes, I will accept my inheritance from you. Not because the money is the most important thing to me, but because there is so much good that I can do with it. The first being to give this beautiful woman right here anything her heart desires. I will honor her as my queen." *As you should have done for my mother,* I thought. "I will make sure she has the best," I said, kissing Tess on the lips.

"Jake, baby, I already have everything I could ever want right here with you."

Brockingburg looked mesmerized as he stared at me and Tess. I could tell he knew the things I said I would do for Tess he should have done for my mother.

"Wow! What you guys have is something rich guys dream of, true love. I feel confident no amount of money will corrupt that for you," Brockinburg said as he headed toward the door. "I don't think I could have spent my life amassing wealth for any better reason than for you two to do with it as you see fit."

I looked at Tess, and she nudged me. I reached out and did something I thought I would never do. I wrapped my arms around my father and embraced him. "Thank you," I said as I pat his back.

He held onto me as if he never wanted to let go.

"No, thank you, Son, for being nothing like me. There was a time when I thought family wasn't important. I'm glad you know that it is," he said and walked to the door with tears in his eyes.

"It was nice to meet you," Tess said.

"I'll never forget this day," my father replied before he walked over the threshold, leaving Tess and me alone.

I didn't know this for sure, but something told me I wouldn't be seeing much more of the old man. This meeting had somewhat of a finality to it as if he were checking off the final things on a bucket list before his time ran out.

"That was beautiful," my future wife said to me, her smile glowing as she stared at me.

"No, what's beautiful is having someone like you by my side. You were wonderful tonight, but you are always wonderful to me," I said to her and sealed it with a kiss.

"I'm glad we met when we did. This has been a special year. I have overcome a bad marriage and you have reconnected with your father. It can only get better from here," Tess assured.

"Well, now we have a few billion ways to make life better," I said. I smiled allowing myself to grasp what had just transpired with my father.

Tess bit down on her lips. Then, she rubbed her fingers together as if she were holding money between them. "That's right. My man is a baller now." She giggled as she kissed my lips. "I guess I've been taken by a billionaire, huh?" she asked, laughing.

"You are too much," I said, laughing along with her. "Yeah, you're taken, and I'm all yours. I can't wait to officially propose, see my ring on your finger, and change your name. Meanwhile, you're mine to claim, to protect and to spoil."

"Oh, can you handle all of this for the rest of your life, caveman?" she purred and bit down on her lips, gazing at me as her eyes fluttered seductively.

"Tess, Bedroom! Now!" I yelled.

THE END

Made in the USA
Columbia, SC
14 December 2019